O9-AIG-703

HAPPY BIRTHDAY,
BABYMOUSE

BY JENNIFER L. HOLM & MATTHEW HOLM

RANDOM HOUSE 🏠 NEW YORK

This is a work of fiction. Names, characters, places, and incidents either are the product of the authors' imagination or are used fictitiously. Any resemblance to actual persons, living or dead, events, or locales is entirely coincidental.

Copyright © 2014 by Jennifer Holm and Matthew Holm

All rights reserved. Published in the United States by Random House Children's Books, a division of Random House LLC, a Penguin Random House Company, New York.

Random House and the colophon are registered trademarks of Random House LLC.

Visit us on the Web!
randomhouse.com/kids
Babymouse.com

Educators and librarians, for a variety of teaching tools, visit us at
RHTeachersLibrarians.com

Library of Congress Cataloging-in-Publication Data
Holm, Jennifer L.
Happy birthday, Babymouse / by Jennifer L. Holm & Matthew Holm. — 1st ed.
   p.   cm. — (Babymouse ; #18)
Summary: Babymouse imagines the biggest, most wonderful birthday party ever for herself and tries to make it happen, but Felicia is planning her own birthday bash for the very same day.
ISBN 978-0-307-93161-0 (trade pbk.) — ISBN 978-0-375-97097-9 (lib. bdg.) — ISBN 978-0-307-97544-7 (ebook)
I. Graphic novels. [1. Graphic novels. 2. Imagination—Fiction. 3. Birthdays—Fiction. 4. Parties—Fiction. 5. Mice—Fiction.] I. Holm, Matthew. II. Title.
PZ7.7.H65Hap 2013 741.5'973—dc23 2012039798

MANUFACTURED IN MALAYSIA   10 9 8 7 6 5 4 3 2 1   First Edition

Random House Children's Books supports the First Amendment and celebrates the right to read.

BABYMOUSE AND FRIENDS*

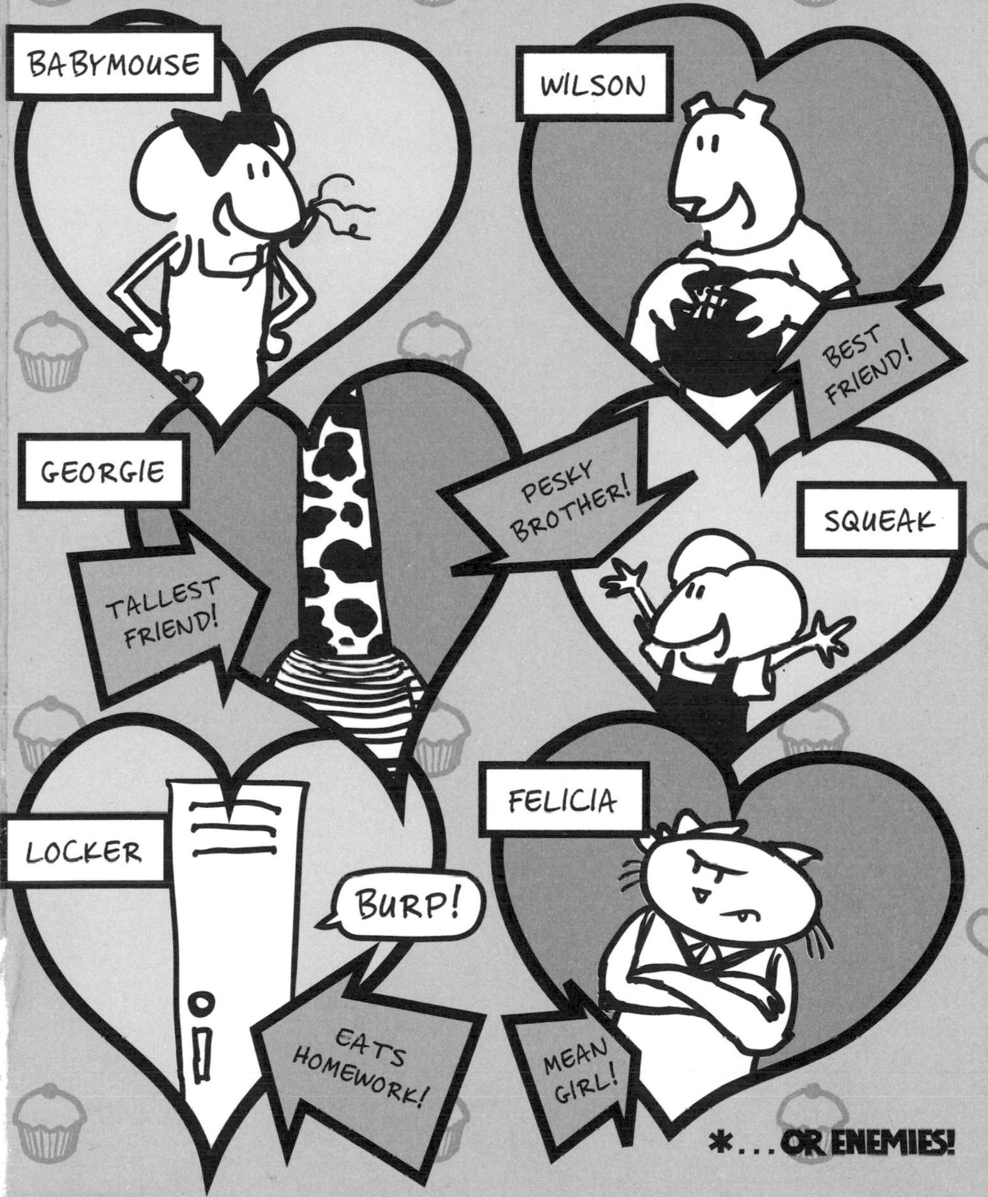
BABYMOUSE
WILSON
BEST FRIEND!
GEORGIE
PESKY BROTHER!
TALLEST FRIEND!
SQUEAK
LOCKER
BURP!
EATS HOMEWORK!
FELICIA
MEAN GIRL!

*...OR ENEMIES!

THEY MAKE THE PERFECT BIRTHDAY GIFT!

BE SURE TO READ **ALL** THE **BABYMOUSE** BOOKS:

#1   BABYMOUSE: Queen of the World!
#2   BABYMOUSE: Our Hero
#3   BABYMOUSE: Beach Babe
#4   BABYMOUSE: Rock Star
#5   BABYMOUSE: Heartbreaker
#6   CAMP BABYMOUSE
#7   BABYMOUSE: Skater Girl
#8   BABYMOUSE: Puppy Love
#9   BABYMOUSE: Monster Mash
#10 BABYMOUSE: The Musical
#11 BABYMOUSE: Dragonslayer
#12 BABYMOUSE: Burns Rubber
#13 BABYMOUSE: Cupcake Tycoon
#14 BABYMOUSE: Mad Scientist
#15 A Very BABYMOUSE Christmas
#16 BABYMOUSE for President
#17 Extreme BABYMOUSE
#18 Happy Birthday, BABYMOUSE

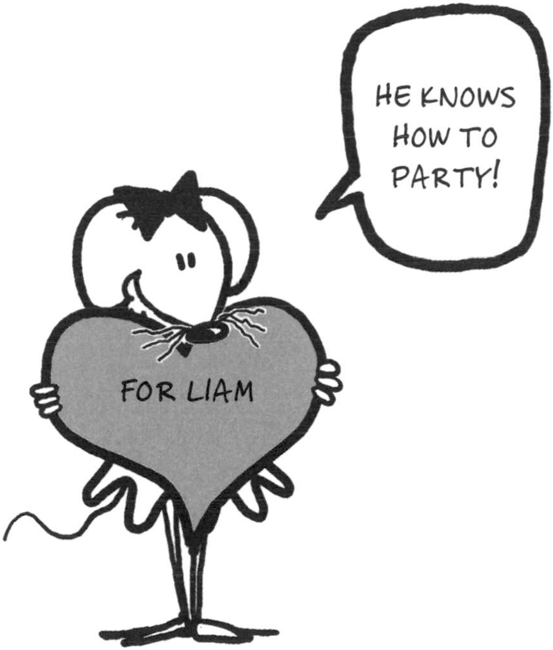
HE KNOWS HOW TO PARTY!
FOR LIAM

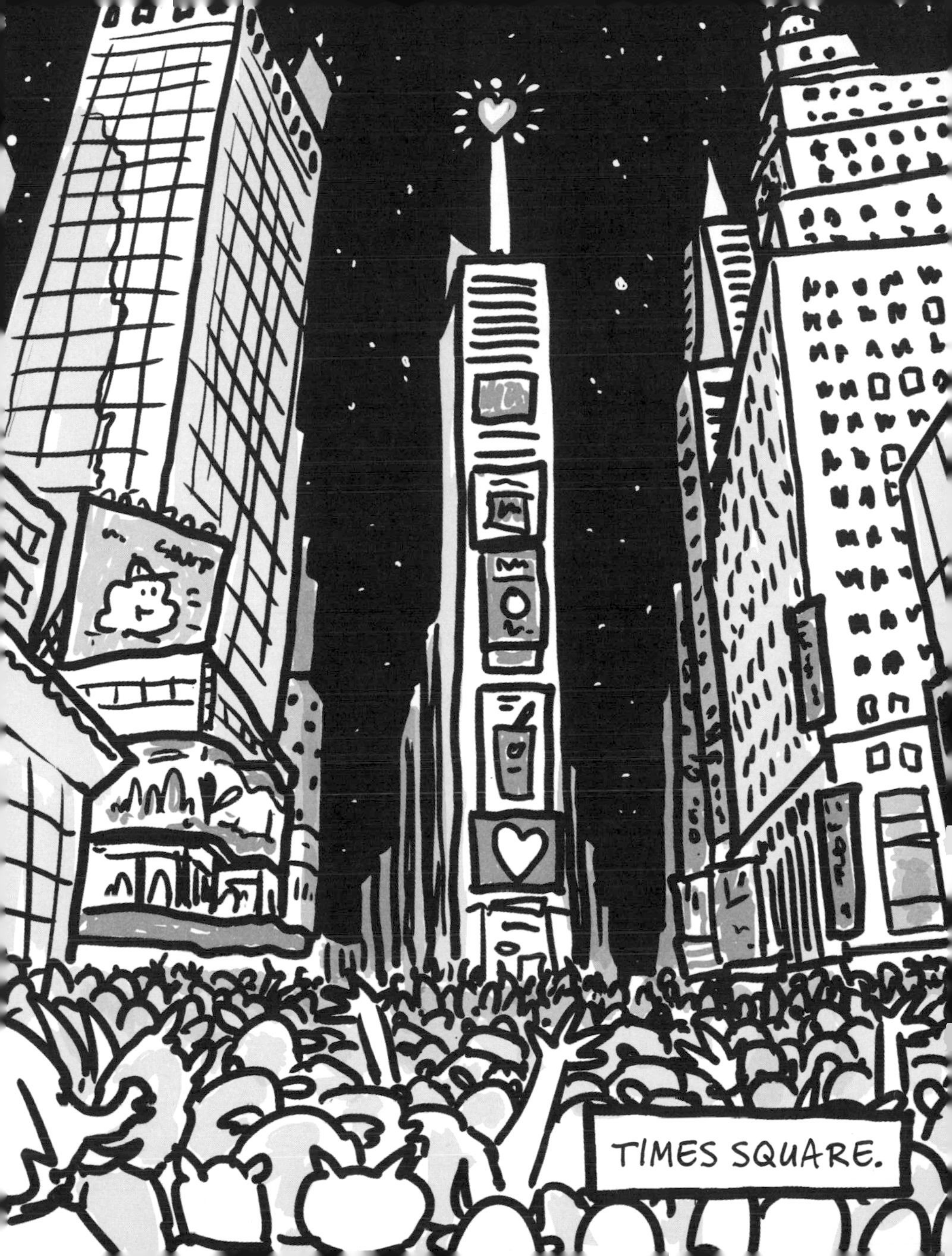
TIMES SQUARE.

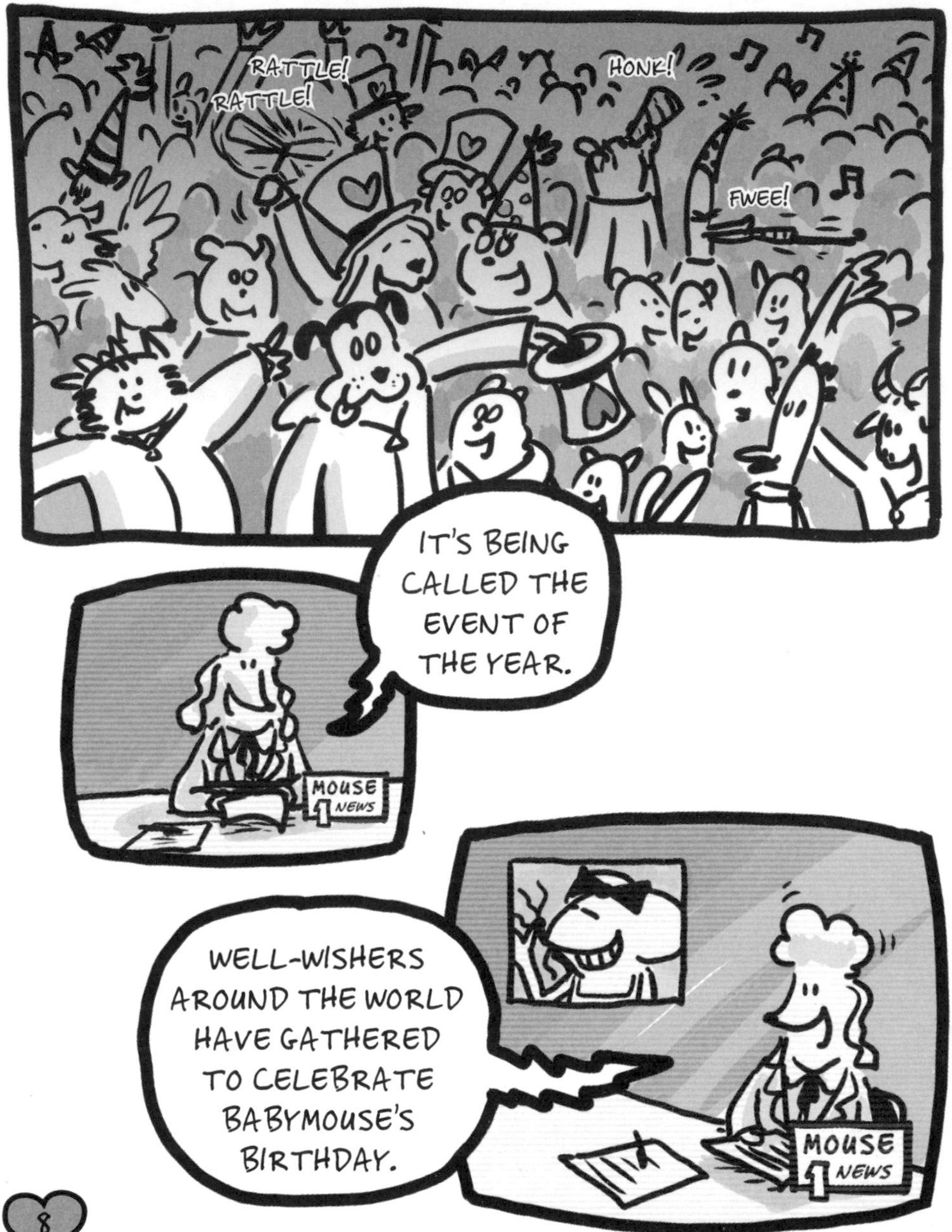
RATTLE!
RATTLE!
HONK!
FWEE!
IT'S BEING CALLED THE EVENT OF THE YEAR.
MOUSE 1 NEWS
WELL-WISHERS AROUND THE WORLD HAVE GATHERED TO CELEBRATE BABYMOUSE'S BIRTHDAY.
MOUSE 1 NEWS

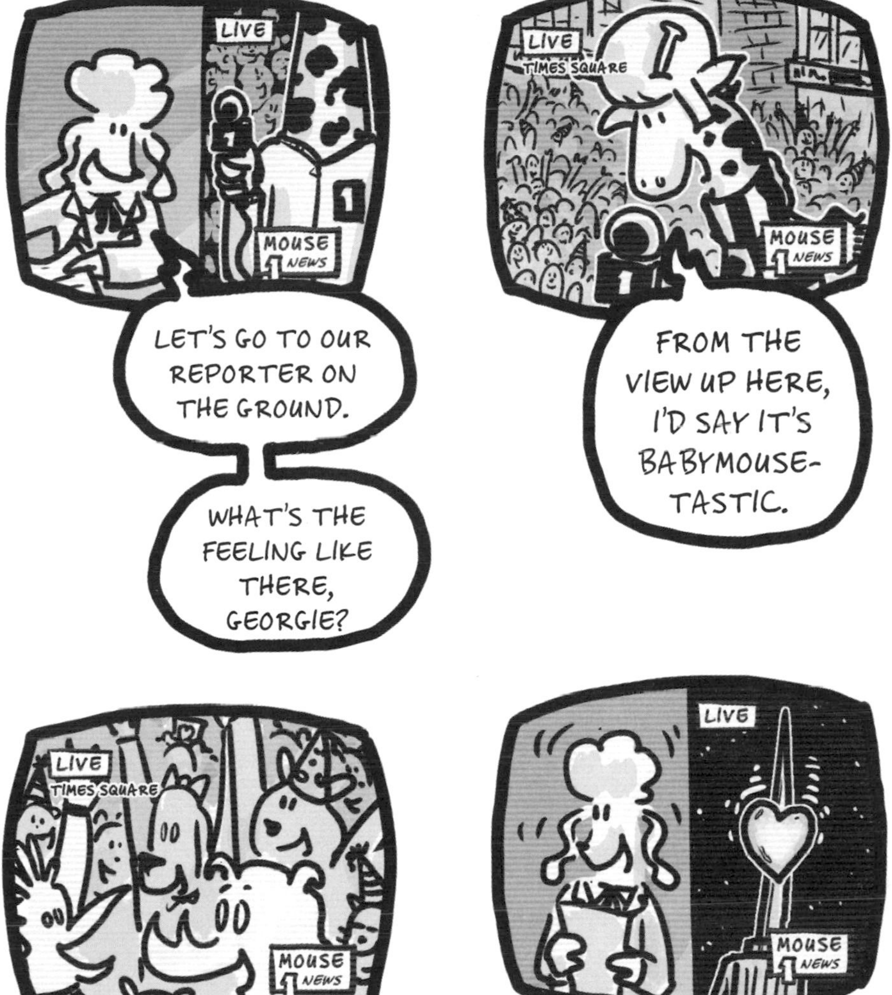
LIVE
MOUSE 1 NEWS
LET'S GO TO OUR REPORTER ON THE GROUND.
WHAT'S THE FEELING LIKE THERE, GEORGIE?
LIVE
TIMES SQUARE
MOUSE 1 NEWS
FROM THE VIEW UP HERE, I'D SAY IT'S BABYMOUSE-TASTIC.
LIVE
TIMES SQUARE
MOUSE 1 NEWS
LIVE
MOUSE 1 NEWS

FIVE . . . FOUR . . . THREE . . . TWO . . . ONE . . .

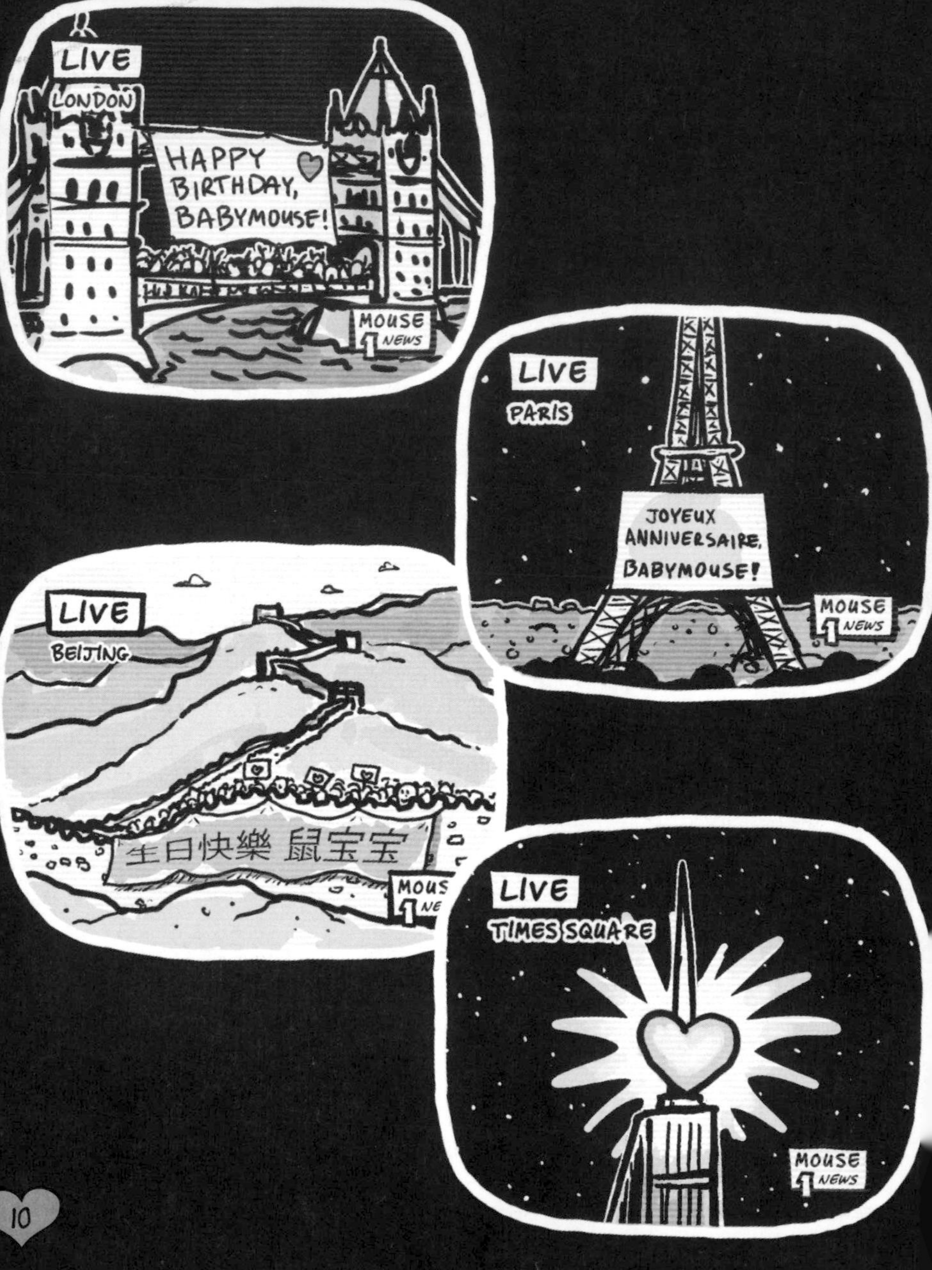
LIVE
LONDON
HAPPY BIRTHDAY, BABYMOUSE!
MOUSE 1 NEWS
LIVE
PARIS
JOYEUX ANNIVERSAIRE, BABYMOUSE!
MOUSE 1 NEWS
LIVE
BEIJING
生日快樂 鼠宝宝
MOUS 1 NE
LIVE
TIMES SQUARE
MOUSE 1 NEWS

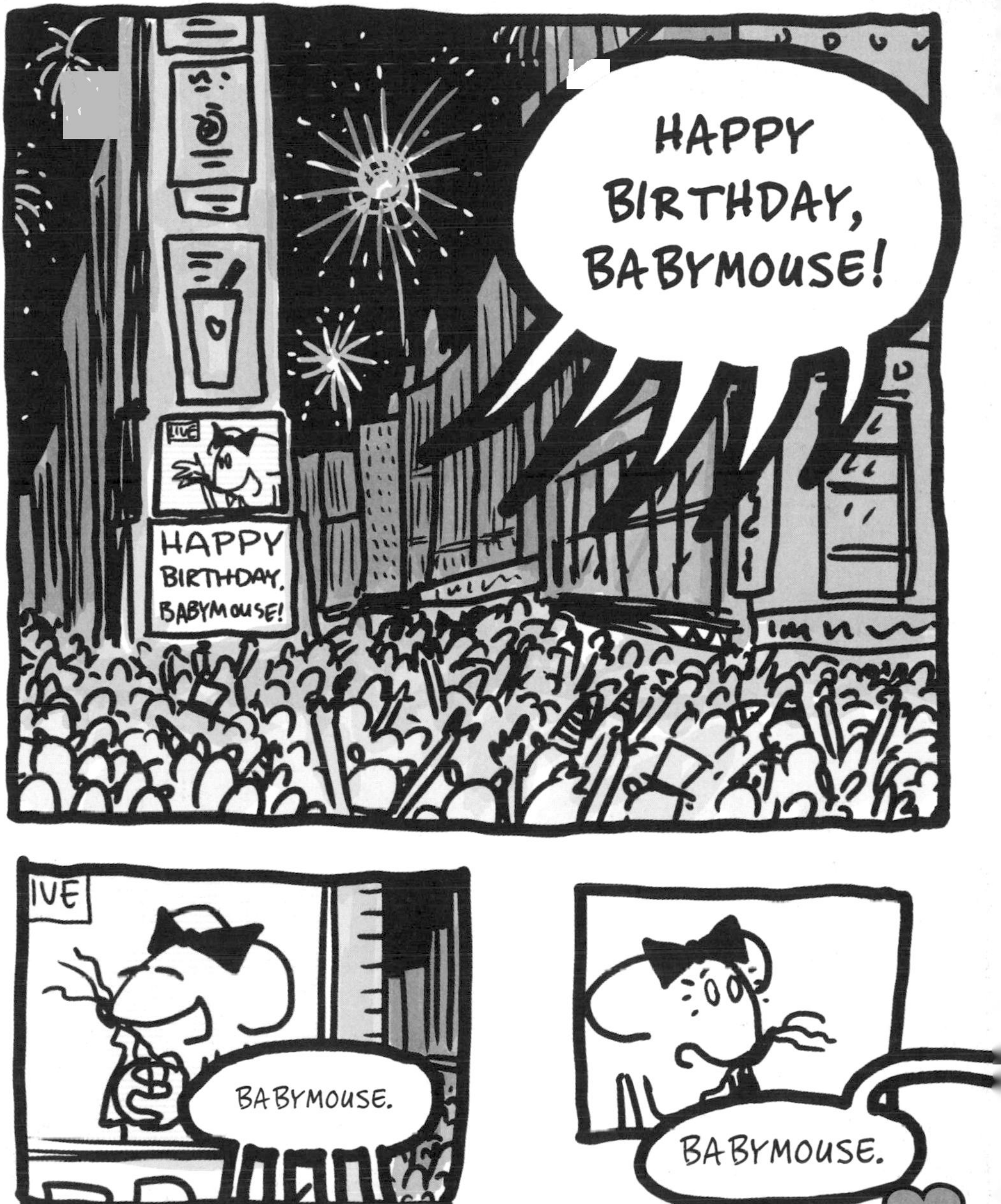
HAPPY BIRTHDAY. BABYMOUSE!
HAPPY BIRTHDAY, BABYMOUSE!
BABYMOUSE.
BABYMOUSE.

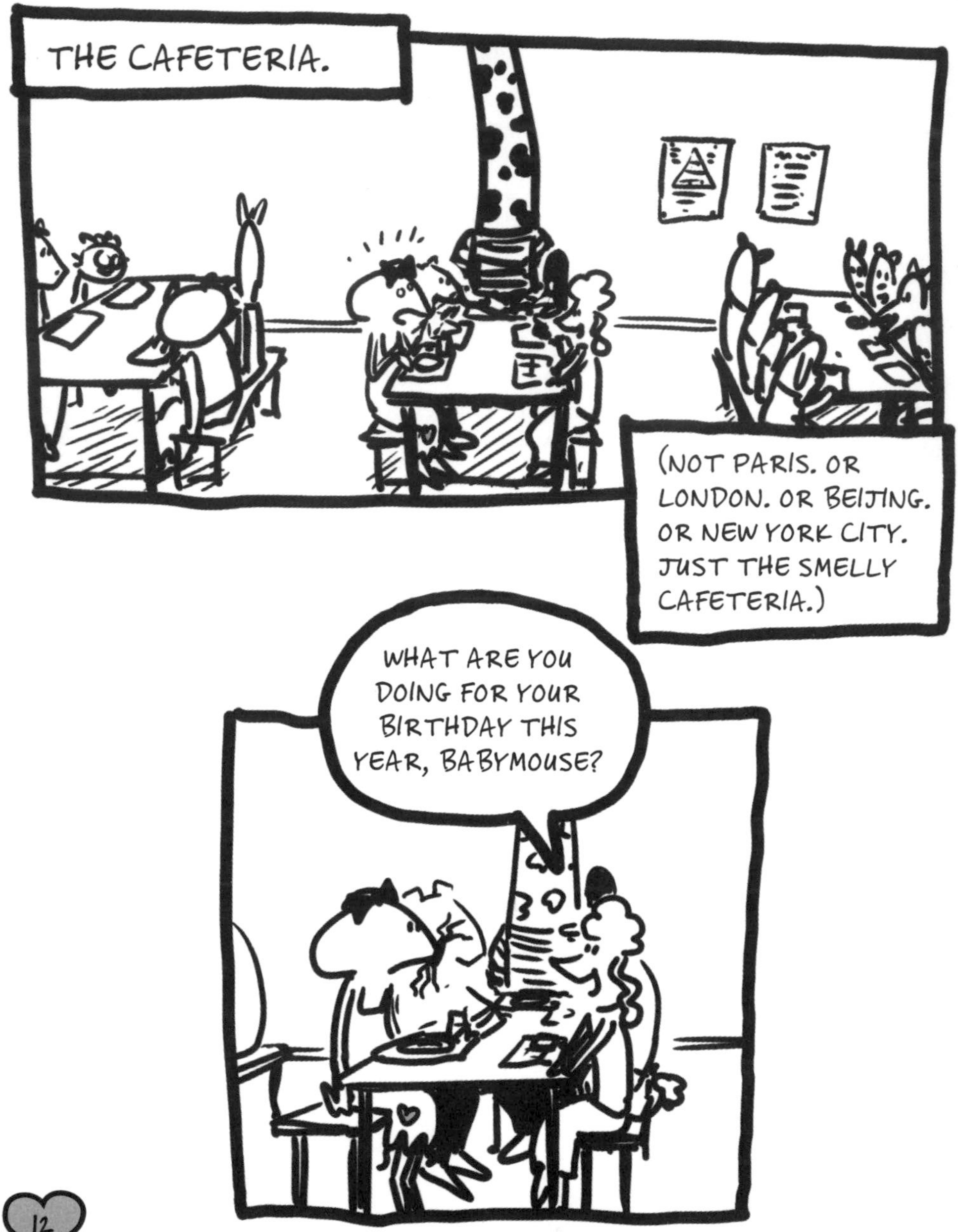
THE CAFETERIA.
(NOT PARIS. OR LONDON. OR BEIJING. OR NEW YORK CITY. JUST THE SMELLY CAFETERIA.)
WHAT ARE YOU DOING FOR YOUR BIRTHDAY THIS YEAR, BABYMOUSE?

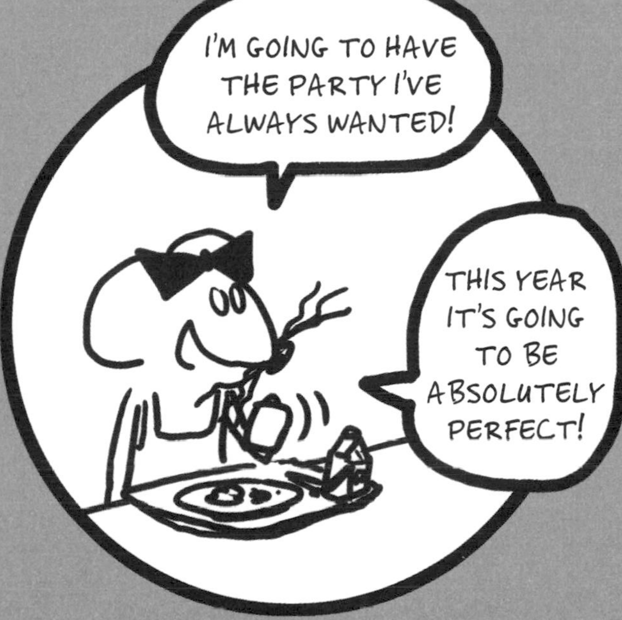
I'M GOING TO HAVE THE PARTY I'VE ALWAYS WANTED!
THIS YEAR IT'S GOING TO BE ABSOLUTELY PERFECT!

LAST YEAR'S BIRTHDAY PARTY.
ZOO
TRUMPET!
AAAGHH!
WAAHHH!!
GRUNT!
AAAAAGH!
ROARRRR!

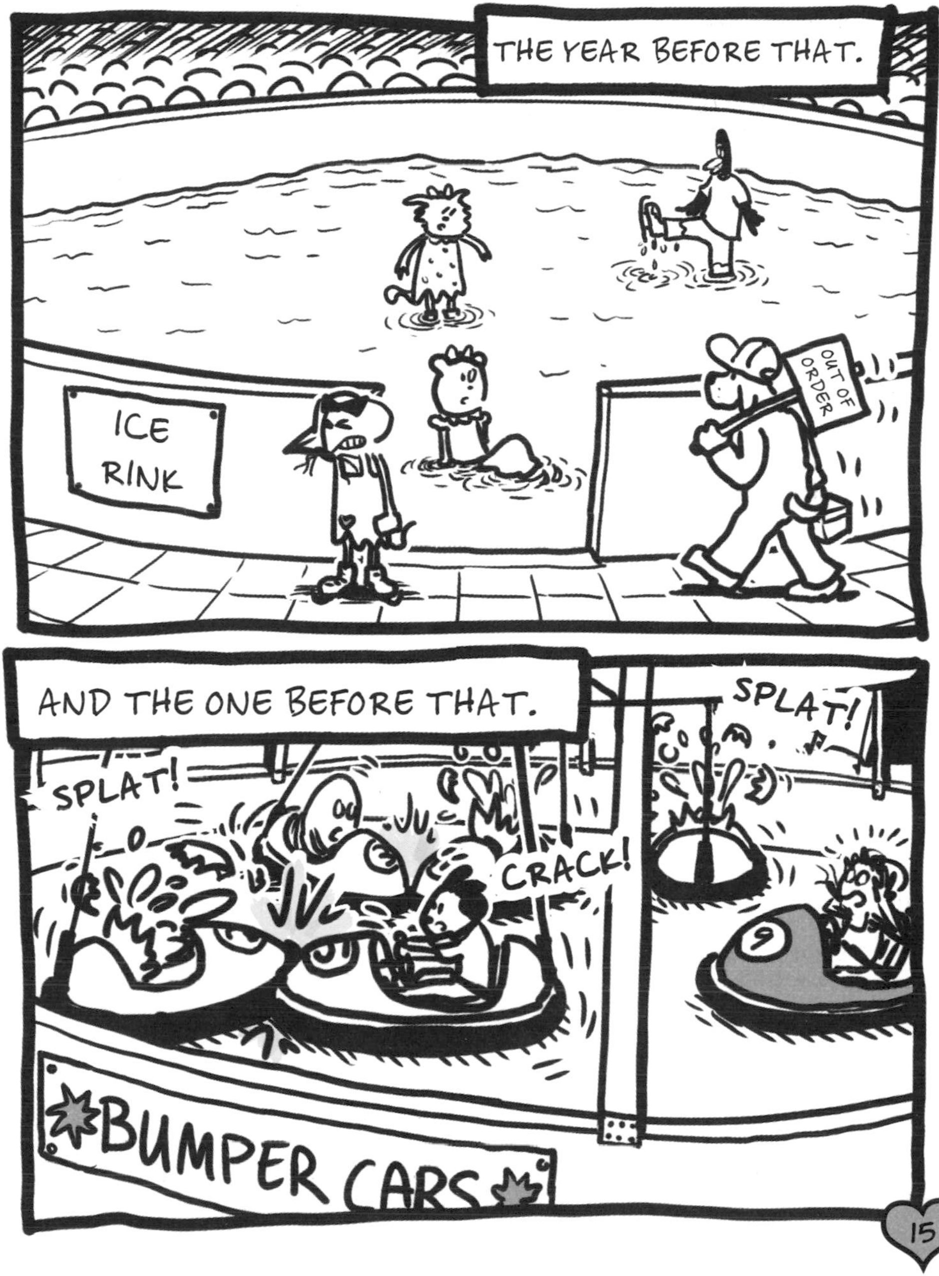
THE YEAR BEFORE THAT.
ICE RINK
OUT OF ORDER
AND THE ONE BEFORE THAT.
SPLAT!
SPLAT!
CRACK!
BUMPER CARS

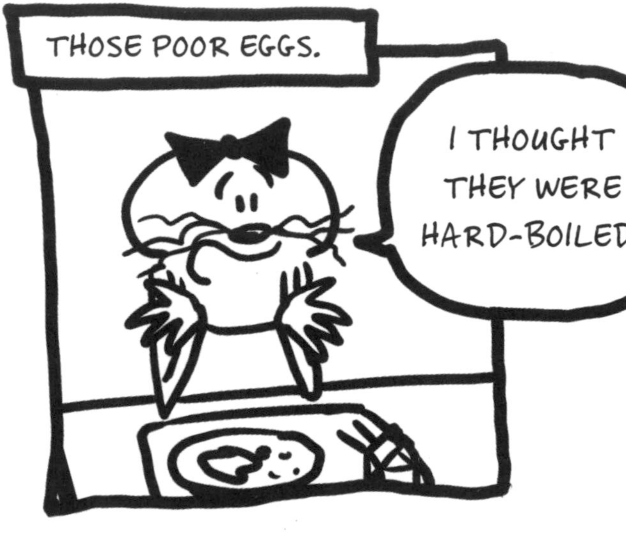
THOSE POOR EGGS.
I THOUGHT THEY WERE HARD-BOILED!

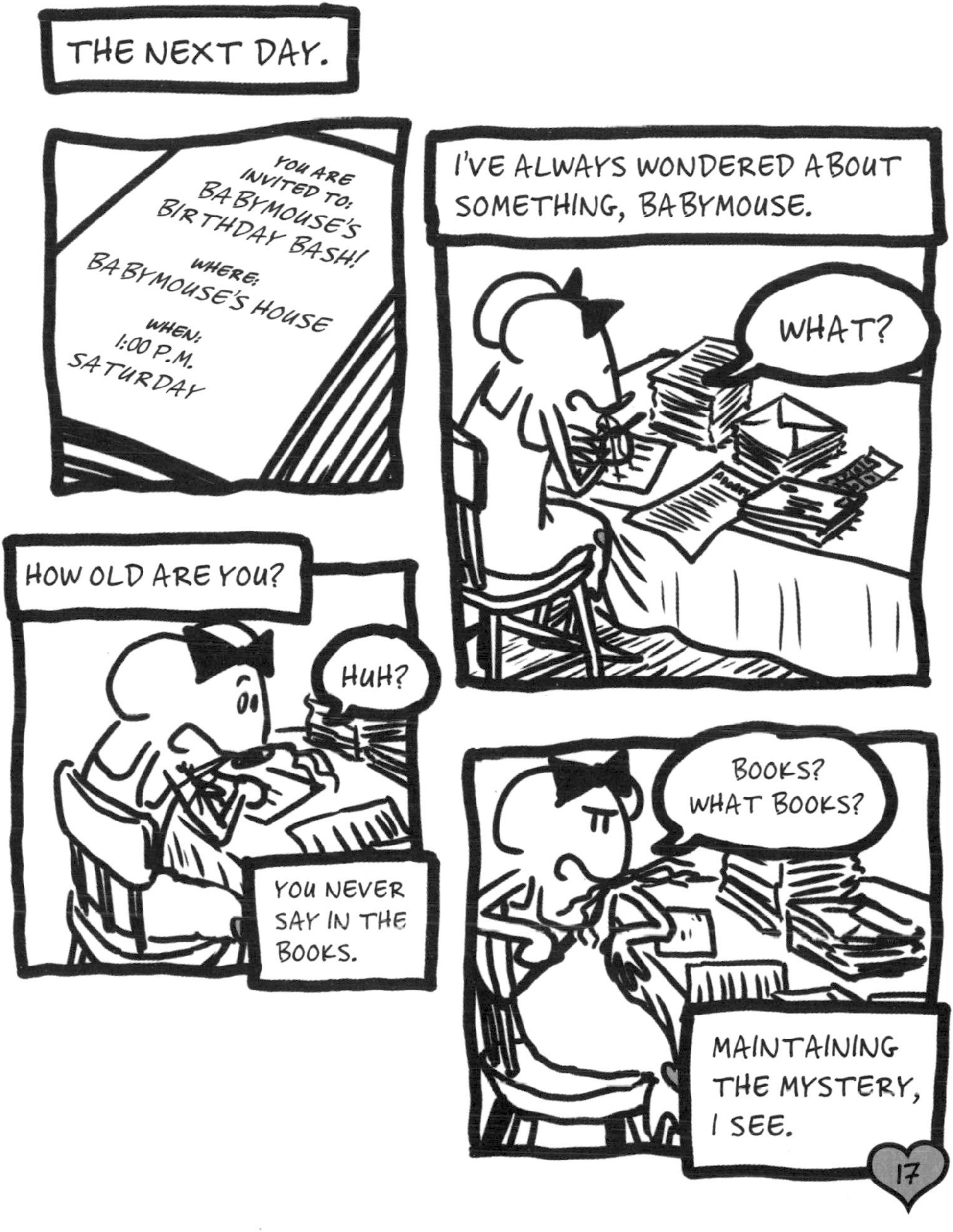
THE NEXT DAY.
YOU ARE INVITED TO: BABYMOUSE'S BIRTHDAY BASH! WHERE: BABYMOUSE'S HOUSE WHEN: 1:00 P.M. SATURDAY
I'VE ALWAYS WONDERED ABOUT SOMETHING, BABYMOUSE.
WHAT?
HOW OLD ARE YOU?
HUH?
YOU NEVER SAY IN THE BOOKS.
BOOKS? WHAT BOOKS?
MAINTAINING THE MYSTERY, I SEE.

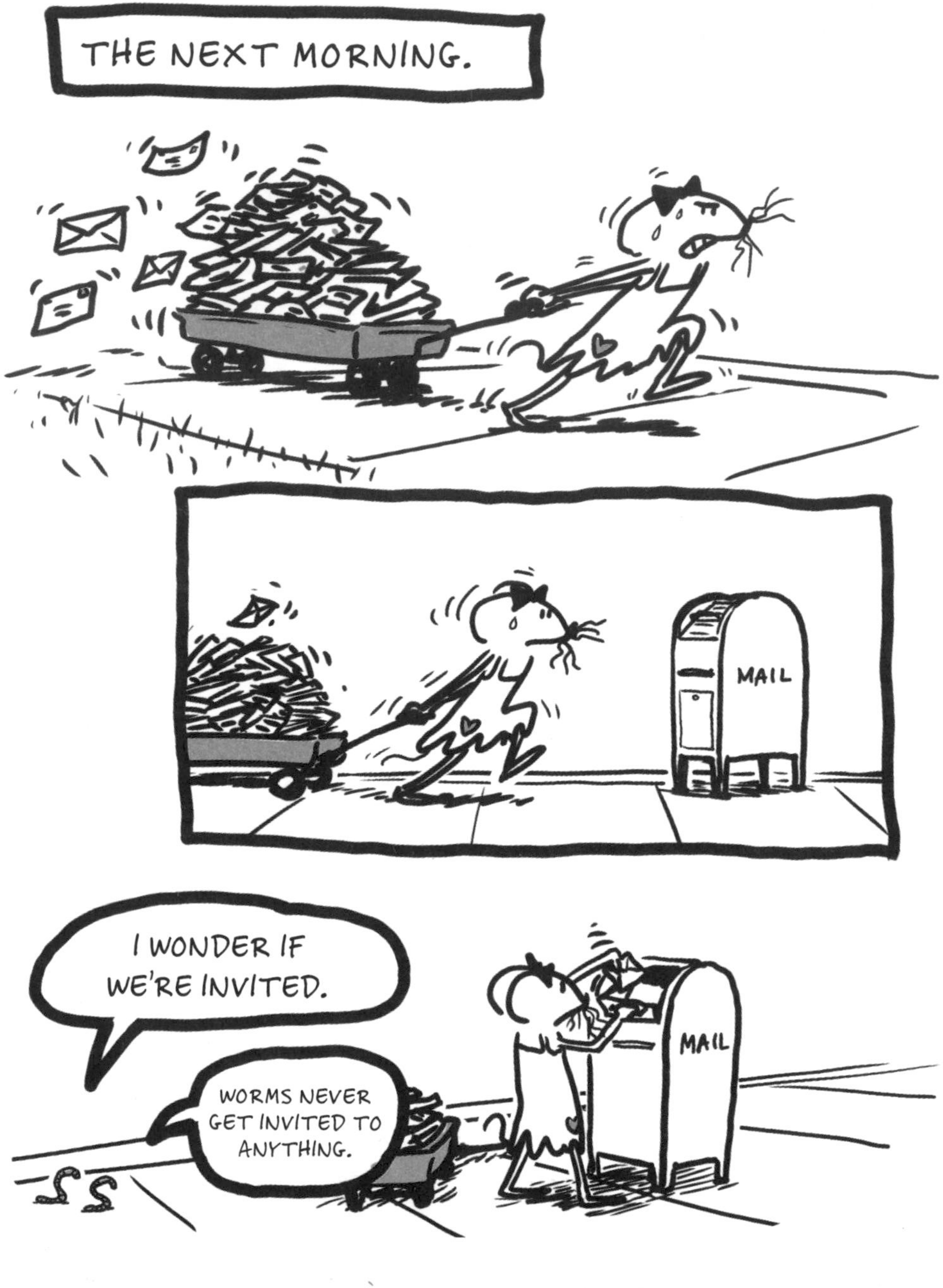
THE NEXT MORNING.
MAIL
MAIL
I WONDER IF WE'RE INVITED.
WORMS NEVER GET INVITED TO ANYTHING.

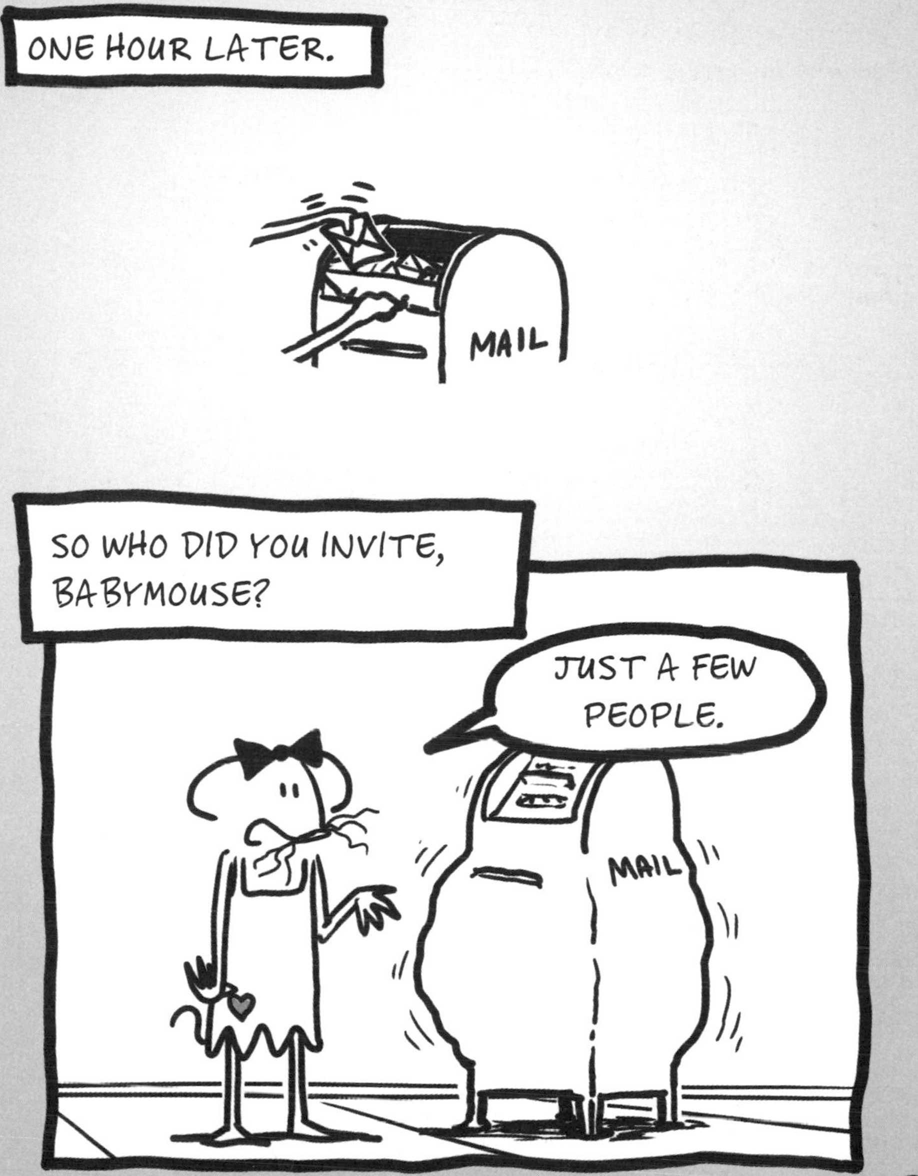
ONE HOUR LATER.
MAIL
SO WHO DID YOU INVITE, BABYMOUSE?
JUST A FEW PEOPLE.
MAIL

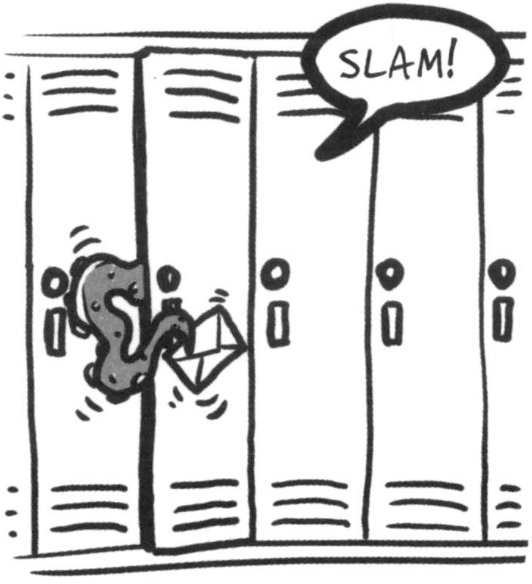
SLAM!

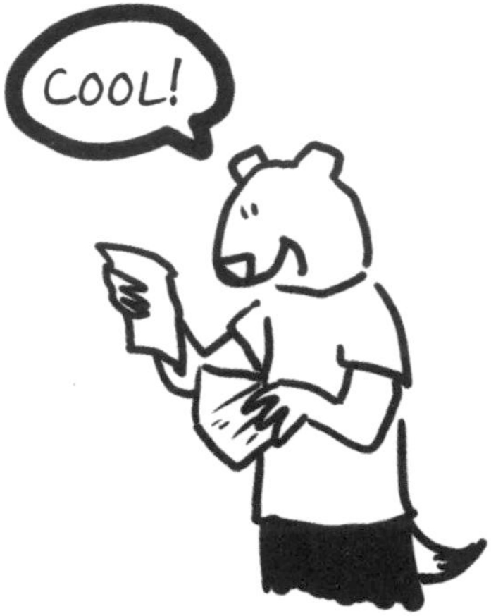
COOL!

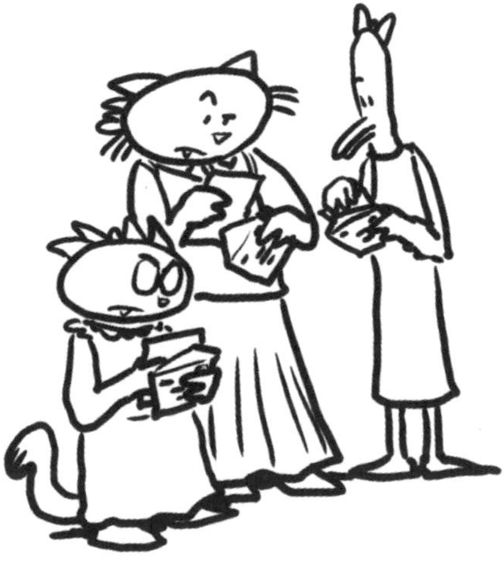

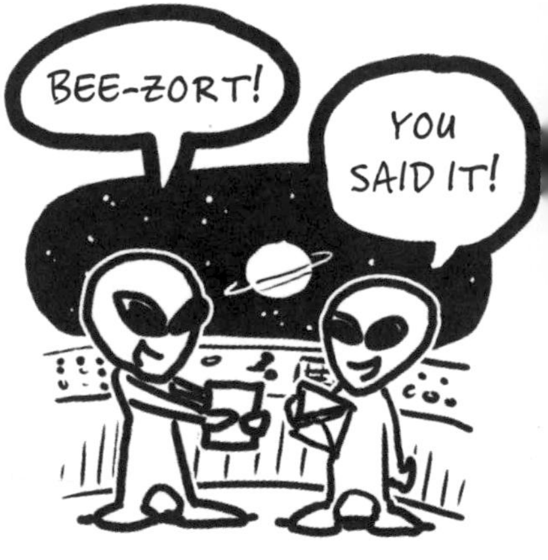
BEE-ZORT!
YOU SAID IT!

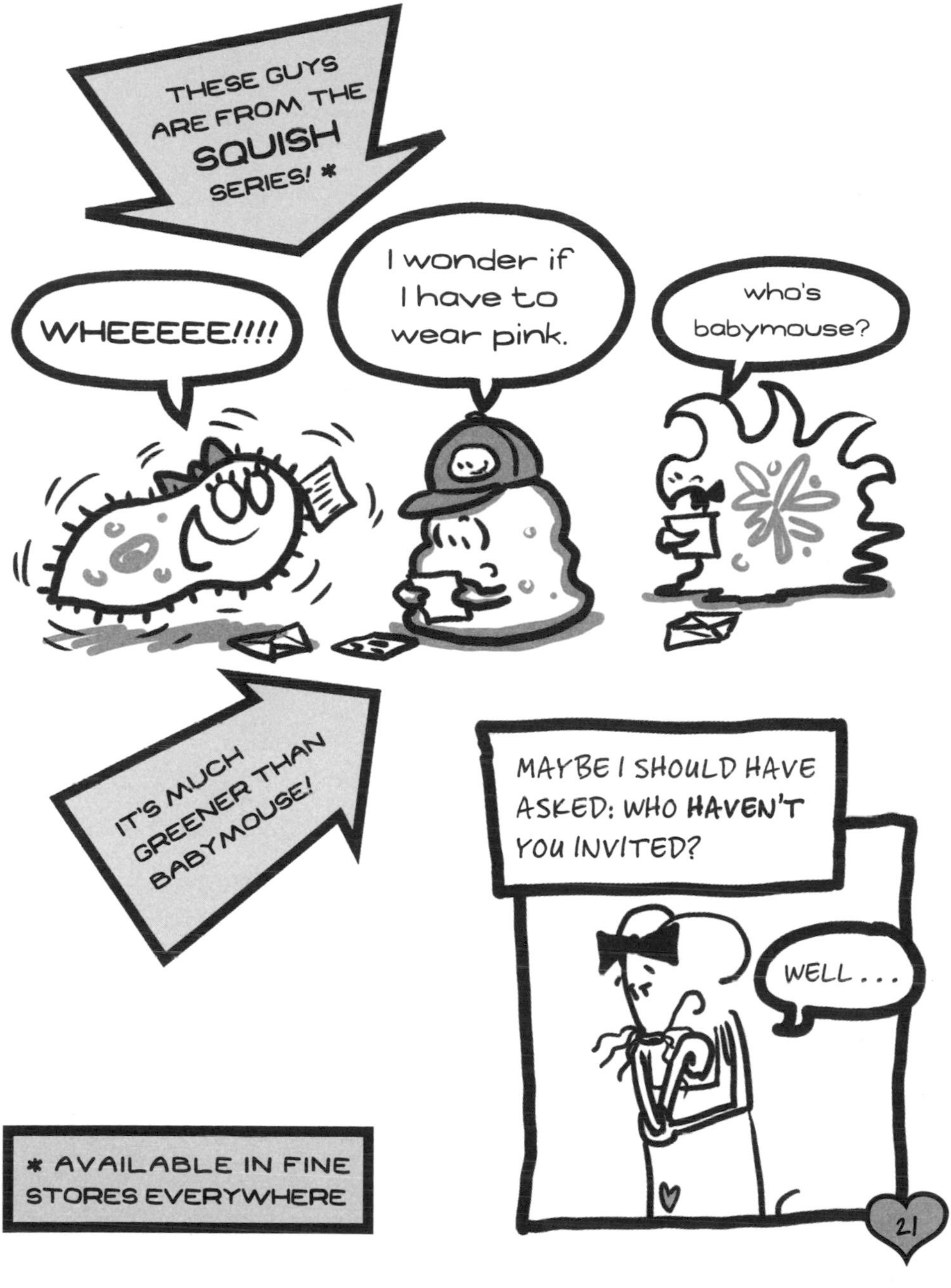
THESE GUYS ARE FROM THE SQUISH SERIES! *
WHEEEEEE!!!!
I wonder if I have to wear pink.
who's babymouse?
IT'S MUCH GREENER THAN BABYMOUSE!
* AVAILABLE IN FINE STORES EVERYWHERE
MAYBE I SHOULD HAVE ASKED: WHO **HAVEN'T** YOU INVITED?
WELL . . .

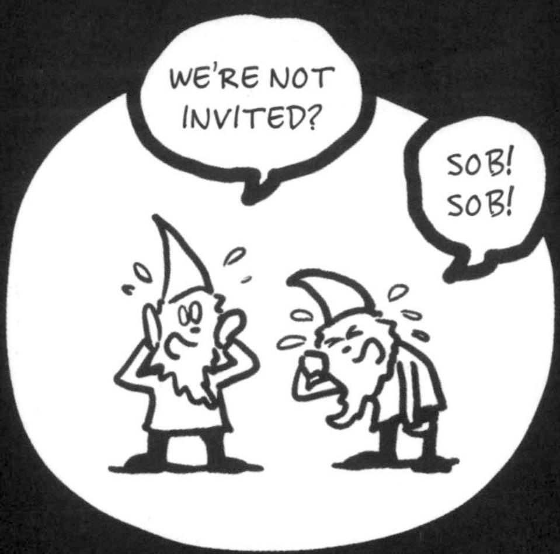
WE'RE NOT INVITED?
SOB! SOB!

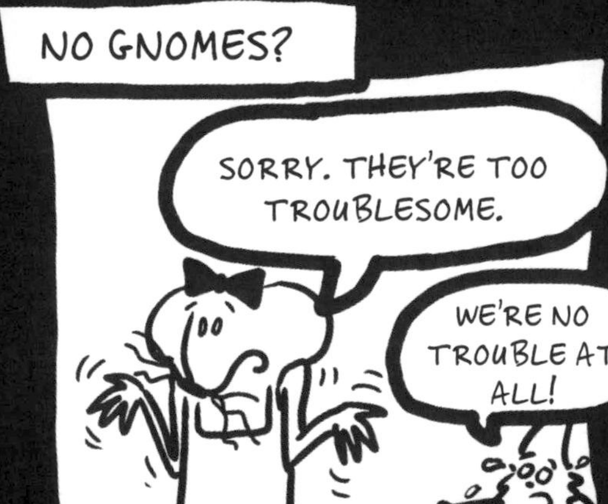
NO GNOMES?
SORRY. THEY'RE TOO TROUBLESOME.
WE'RE NO TROUBLE AT ALL!

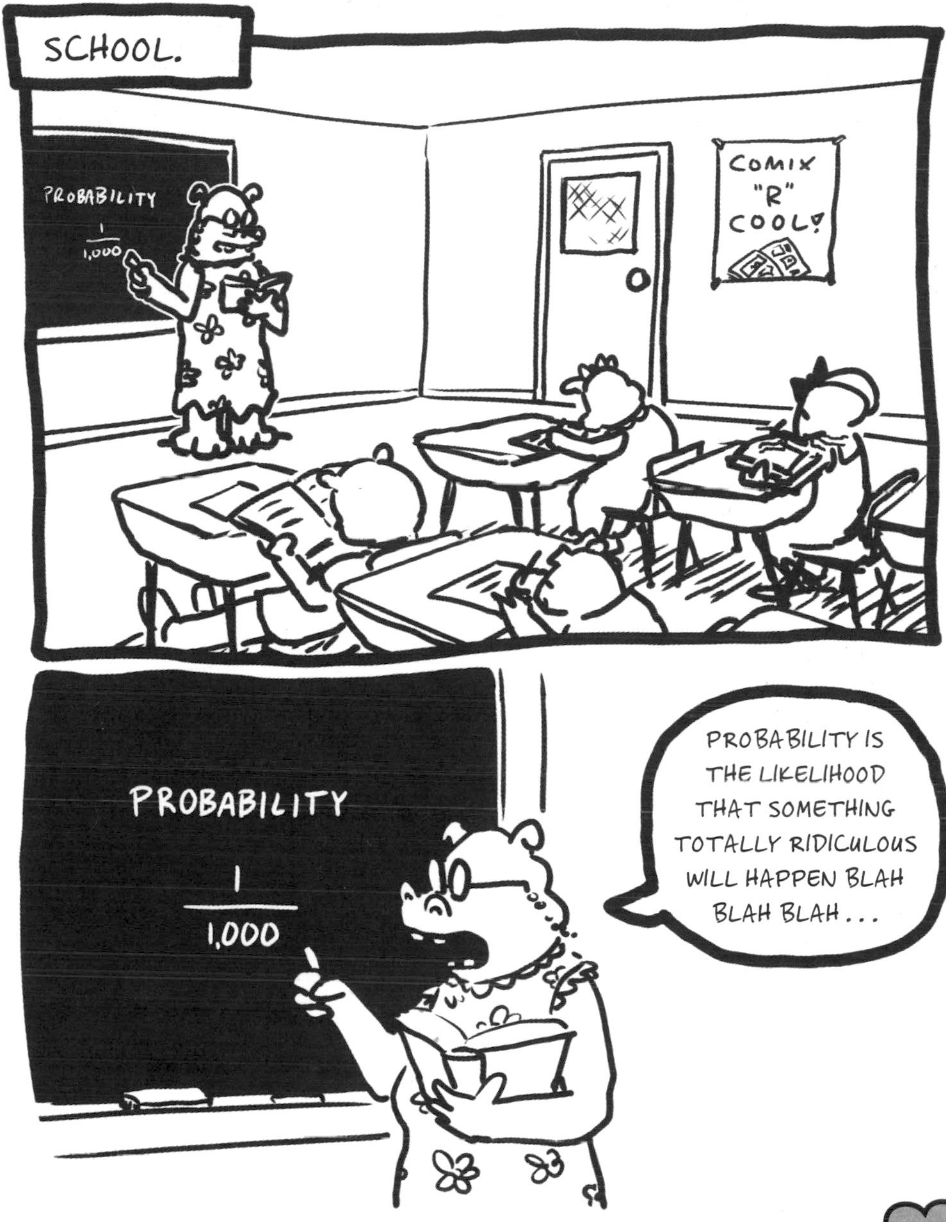
SCHOOL.
PROBABILITY
1
1,000
COMIX "R" COOL!
PROBABILITY
1
1,000
PROBABILITY IS THE LIKELIHOOD THAT SOMETHING TOTALLY RIDICULOUS WILL HAPPEN BLAH BLAH BLAH . . .

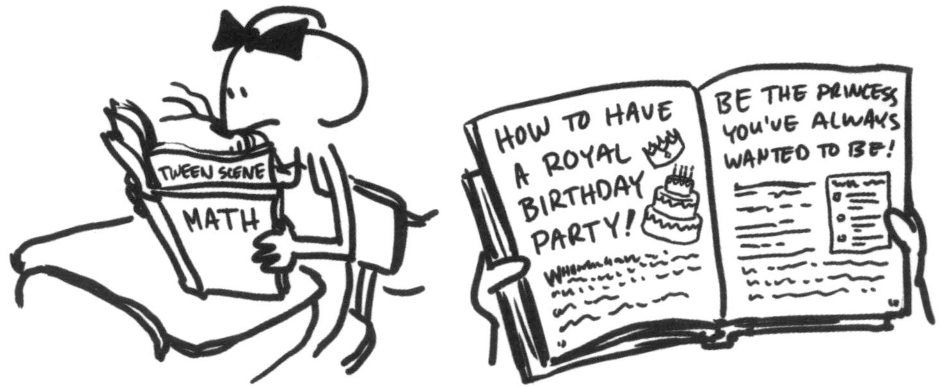
TWEEN SCENE
MATH
HOW TO HAVE A ROYAL BIRTHDAY PARTY!
BE THE PRINCESS YOU'VE ALWAYS WANTED TO BE!

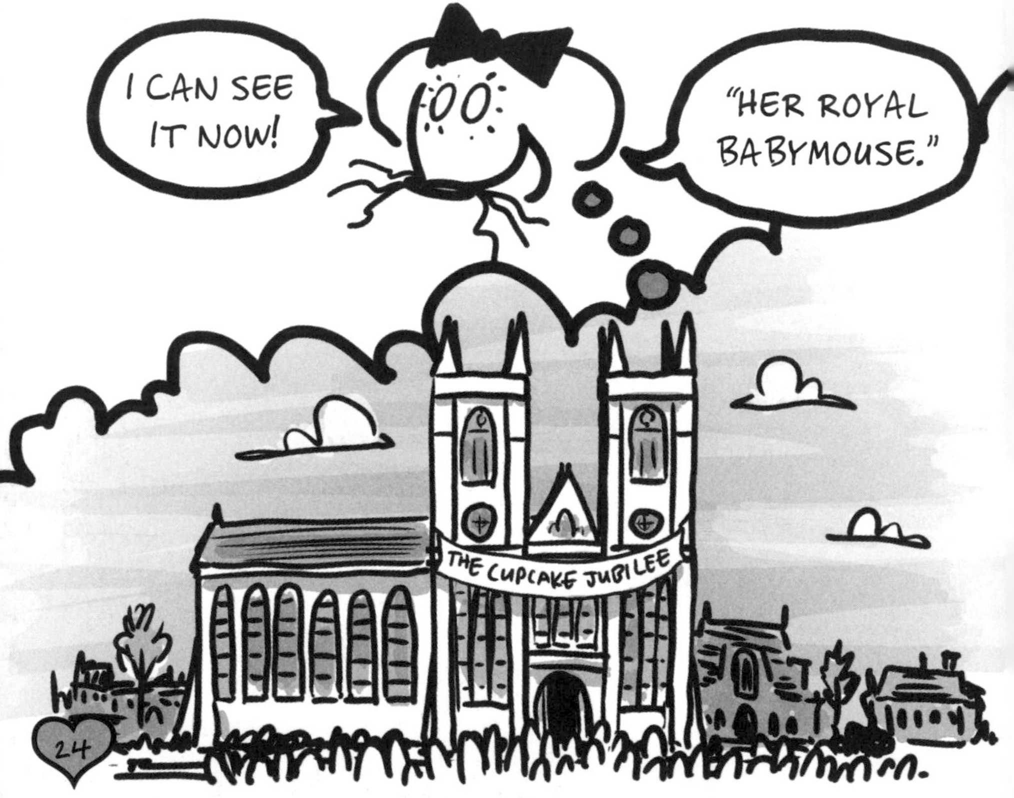
I CAN SEE IT NOW!
"HER ROYAL BABYMOUSE."
THE CUPCAKE JUBILEE

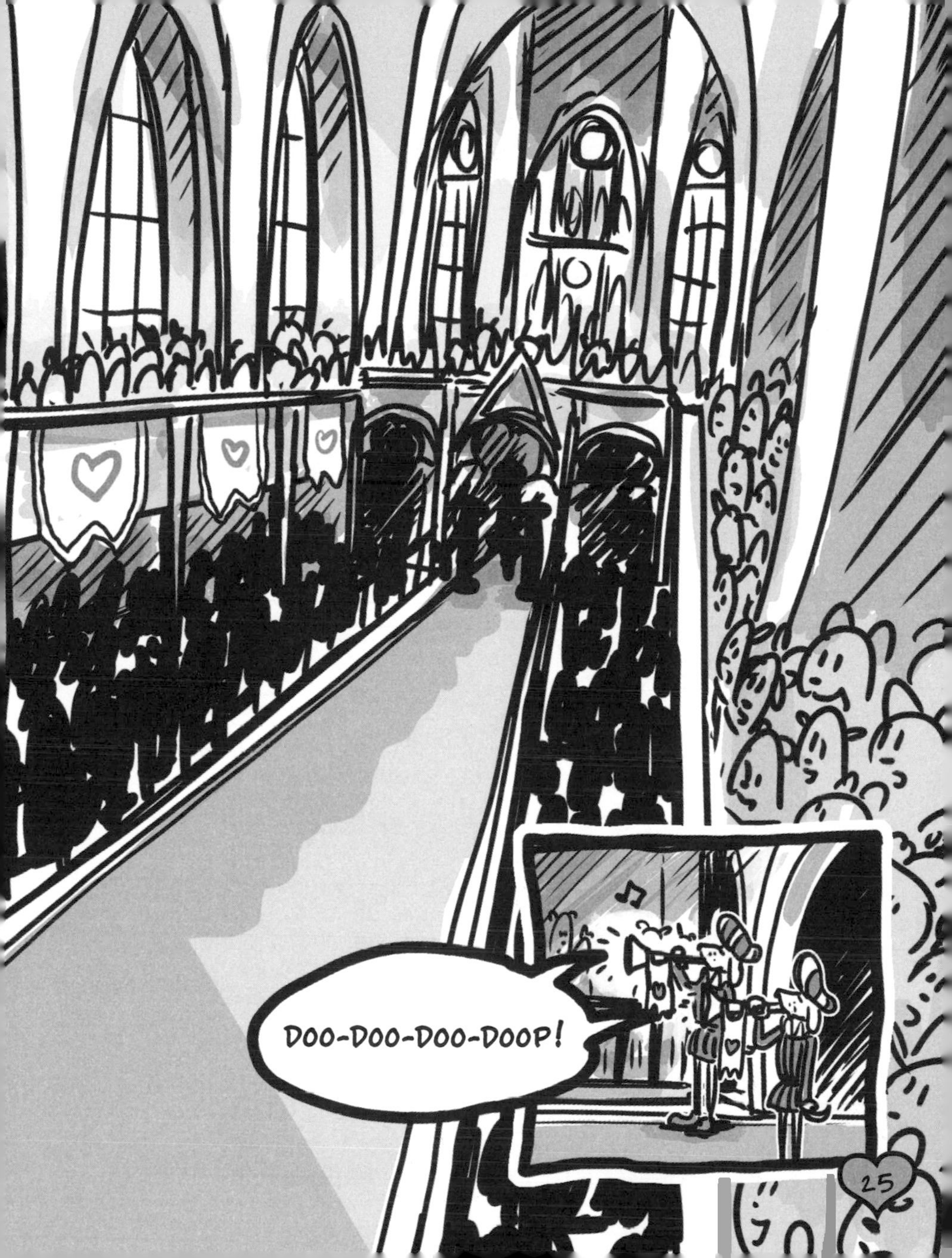
DOO-DOO-DOO-DOOP!

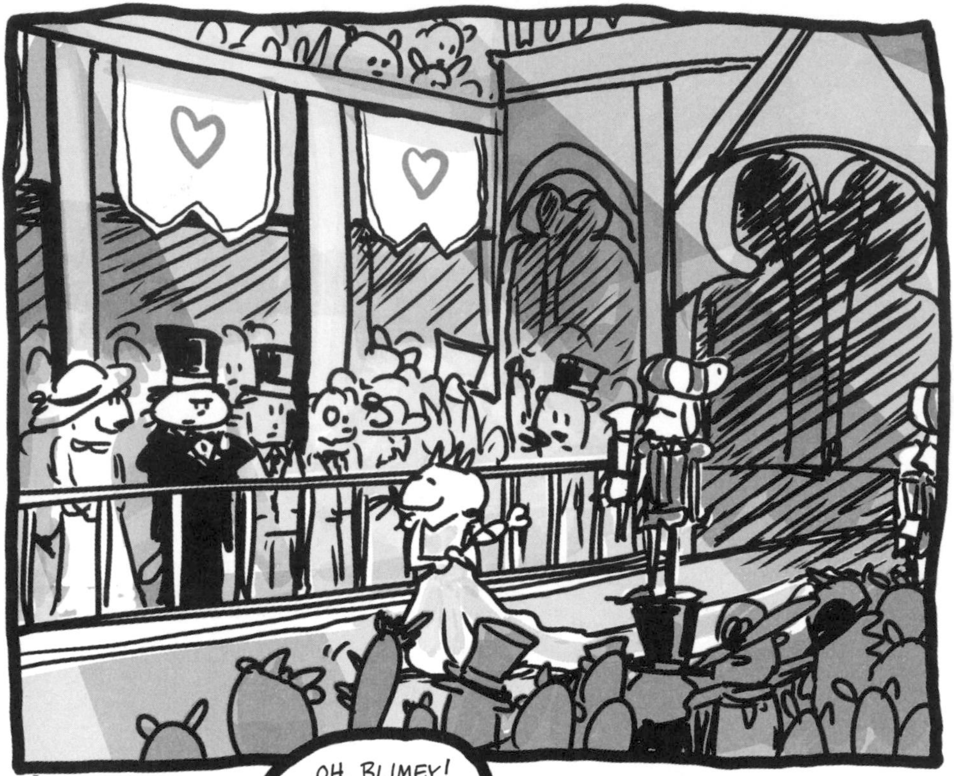

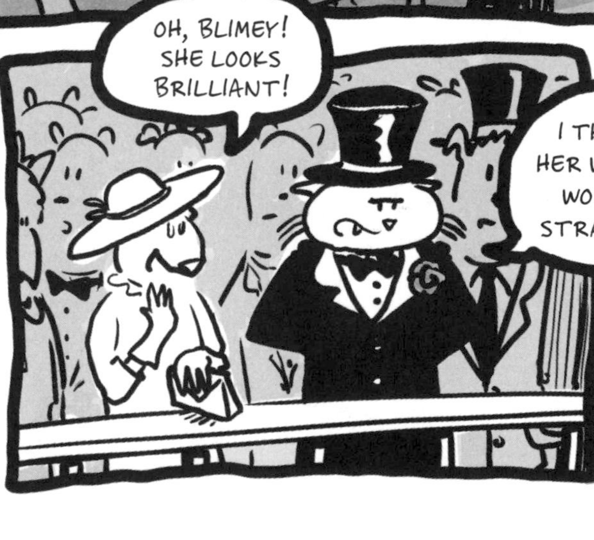
OH, BLIMEY! SHE LOOKS BRILLIANT!
I THOUGHT HER WHISKERS WOULD BE STRAIGHTER.

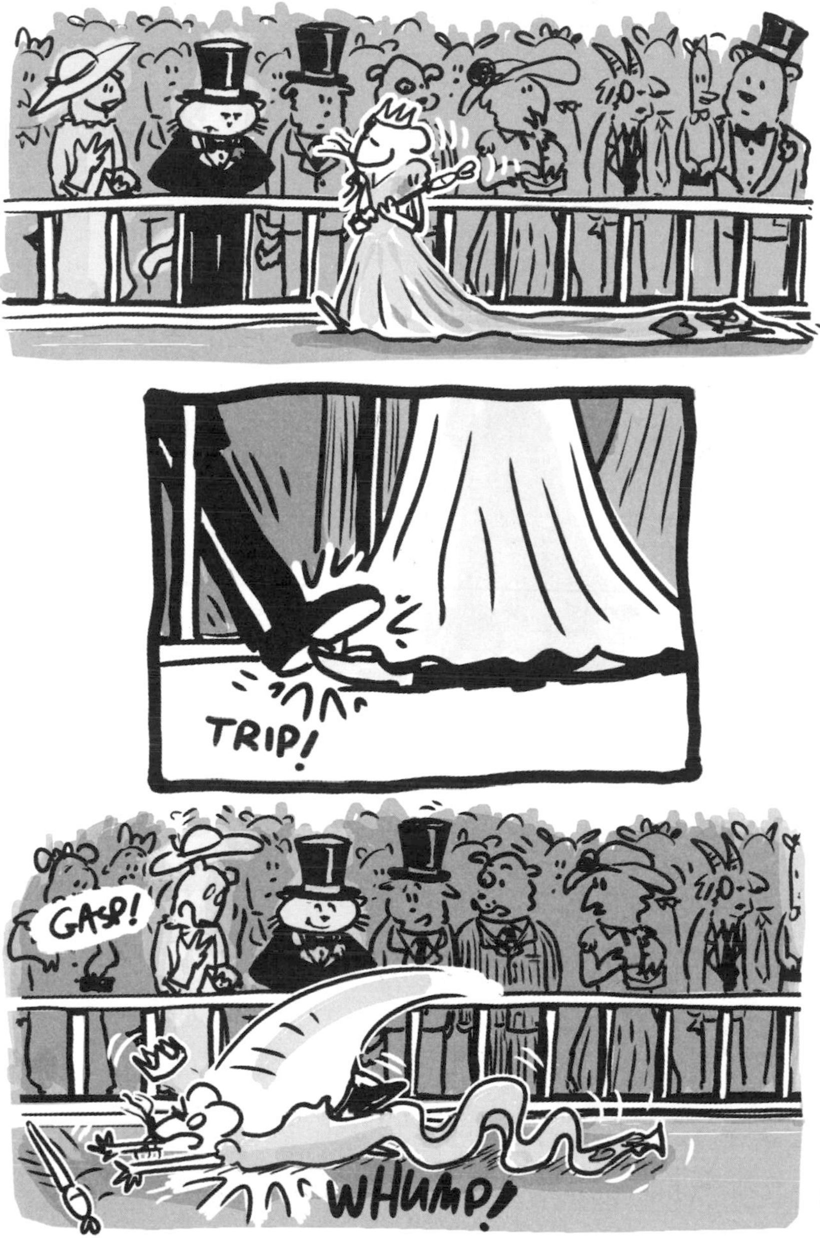
TRIP!
GASP!
WHUMP!

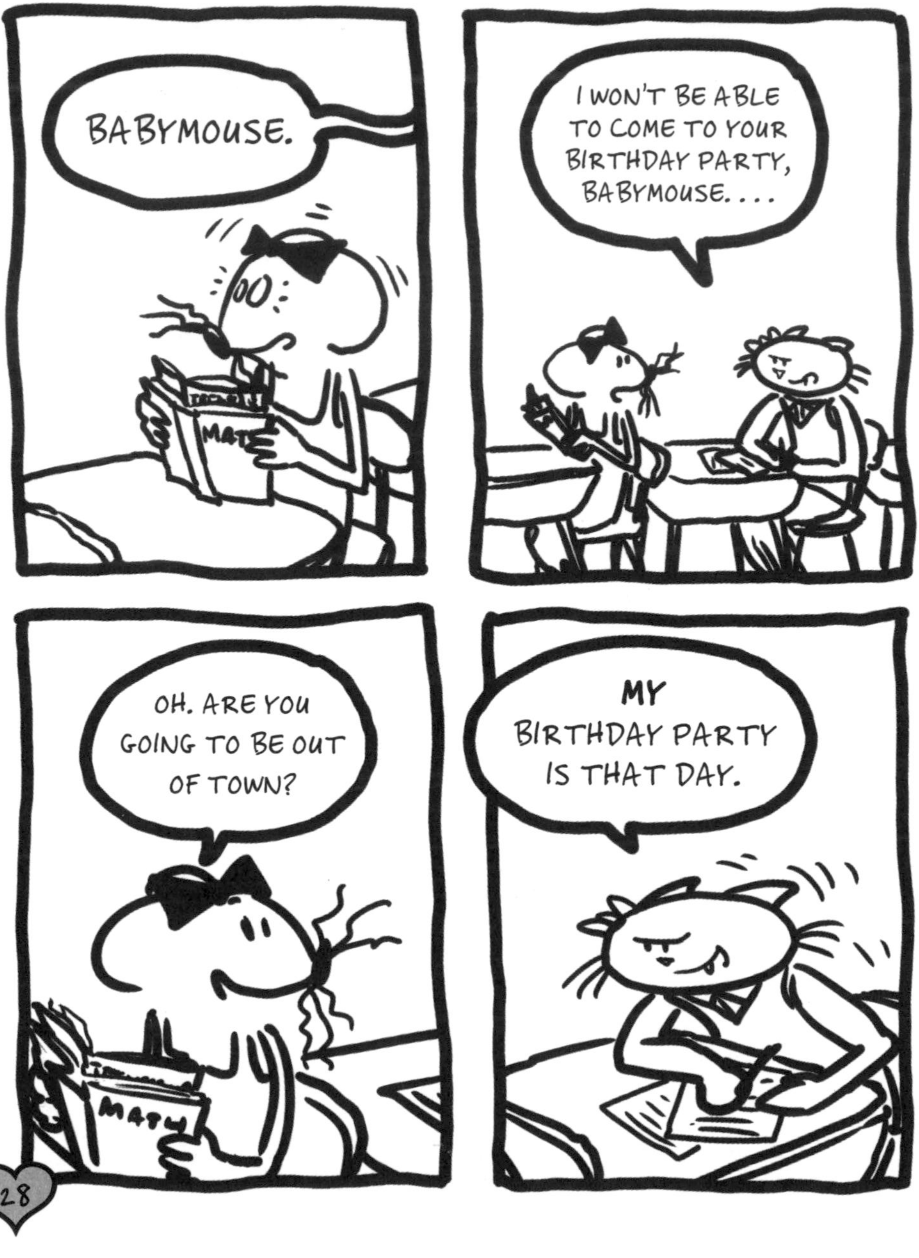
BABYMOUSE.
I WON'T BE ABLE TO COME TO YOUR BIRTHDAY PARTY, BABYMOUSE. . . .
MATH
OH. ARE YOU GOING TO BE OUT OF TOWN?
MATH
MY BIRTHDAY PARTY IS THAT DAY.

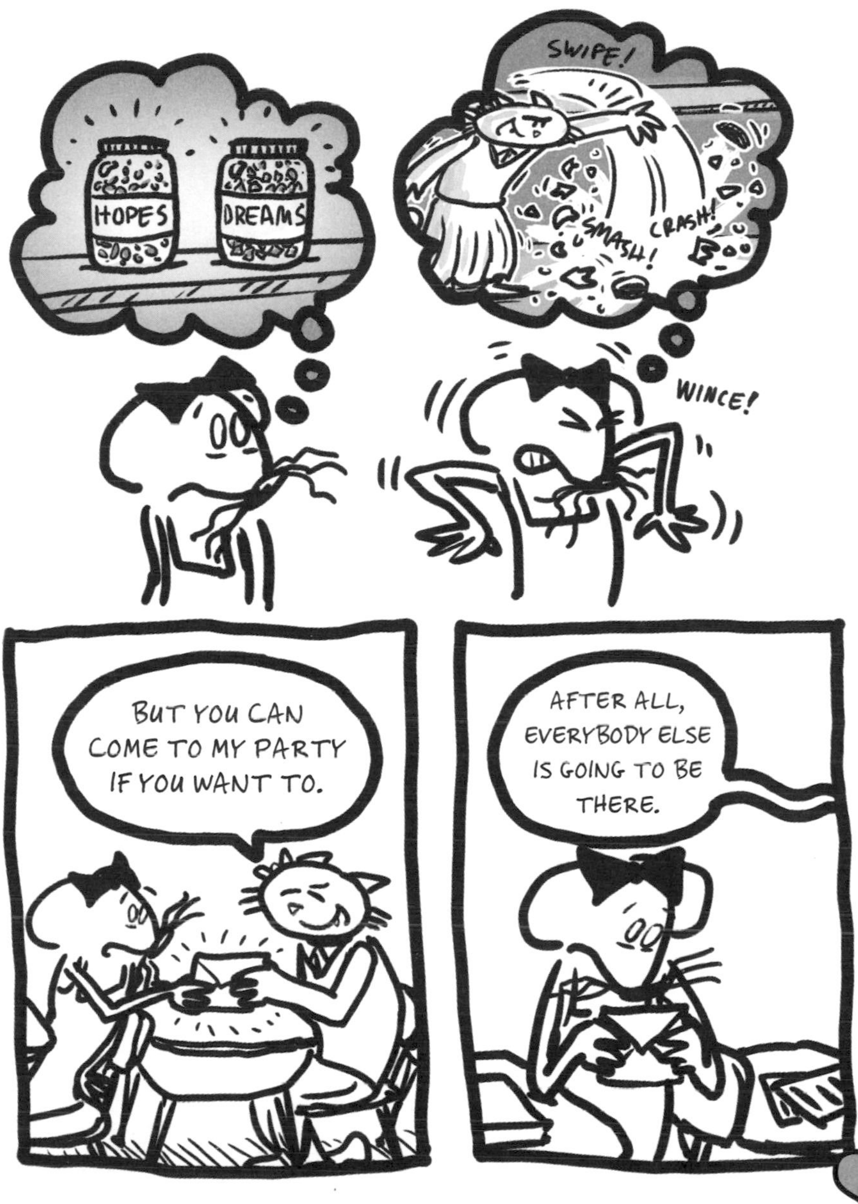
HOPES
DREAMS
SWIPE!
SMASH!
CRASH!
WINCE!
BUT YOU CAN COME TO MY PARTY IF YOU WANT TO.
AFTER ALL, EVERYBODY ELSE IS GOING TO BE THERE.

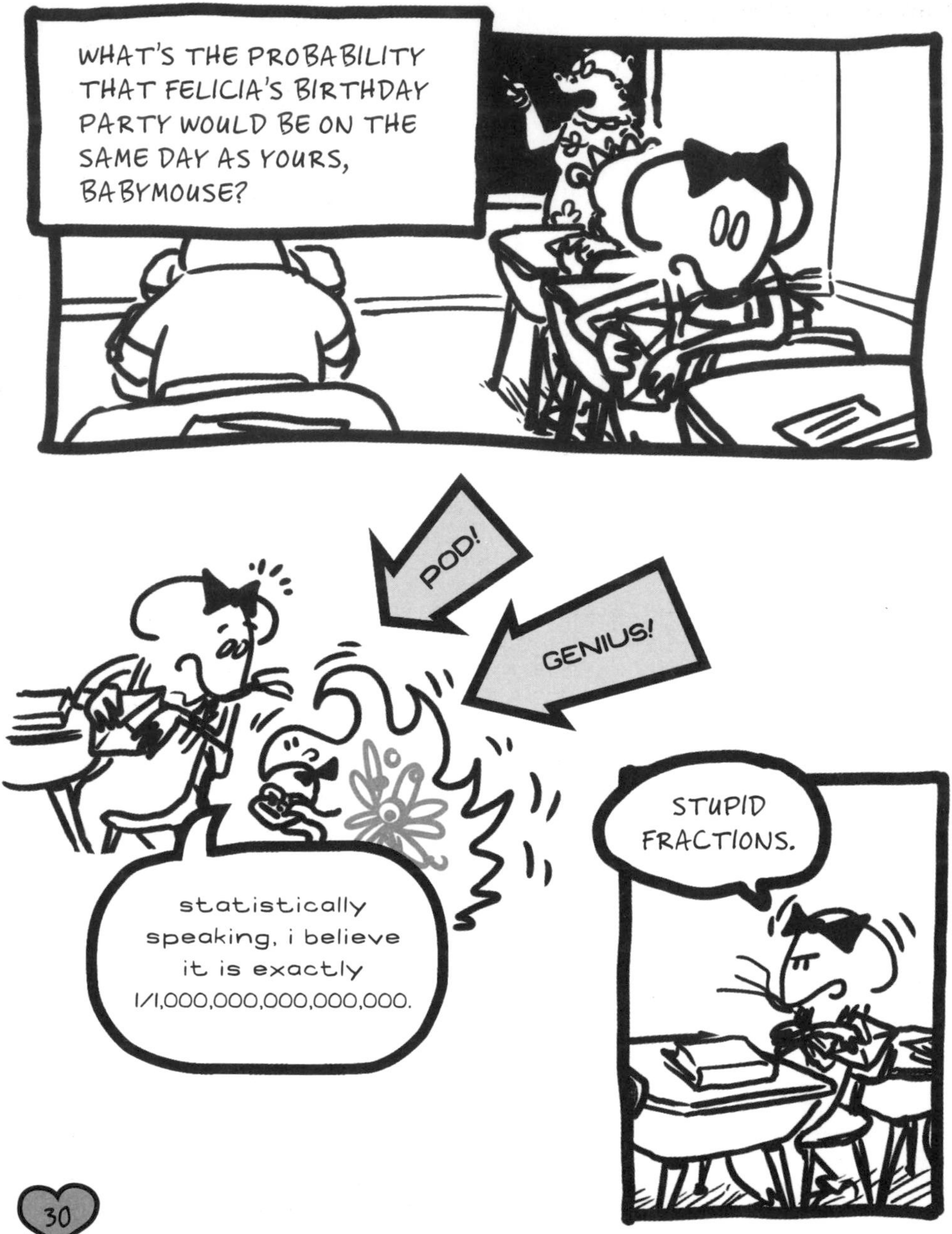
WHAT'S THE PROBABILITY THAT FELICIA'S BIRTHDAY PARTY WOULD BE ON THE SAME DAY AS YOURS, BABYMOUSE?
POD!
GENIUS!
statistically speaking, i believe it is exactly 1/1,000,000,000,000,000.
STUPID FRACTIONS.

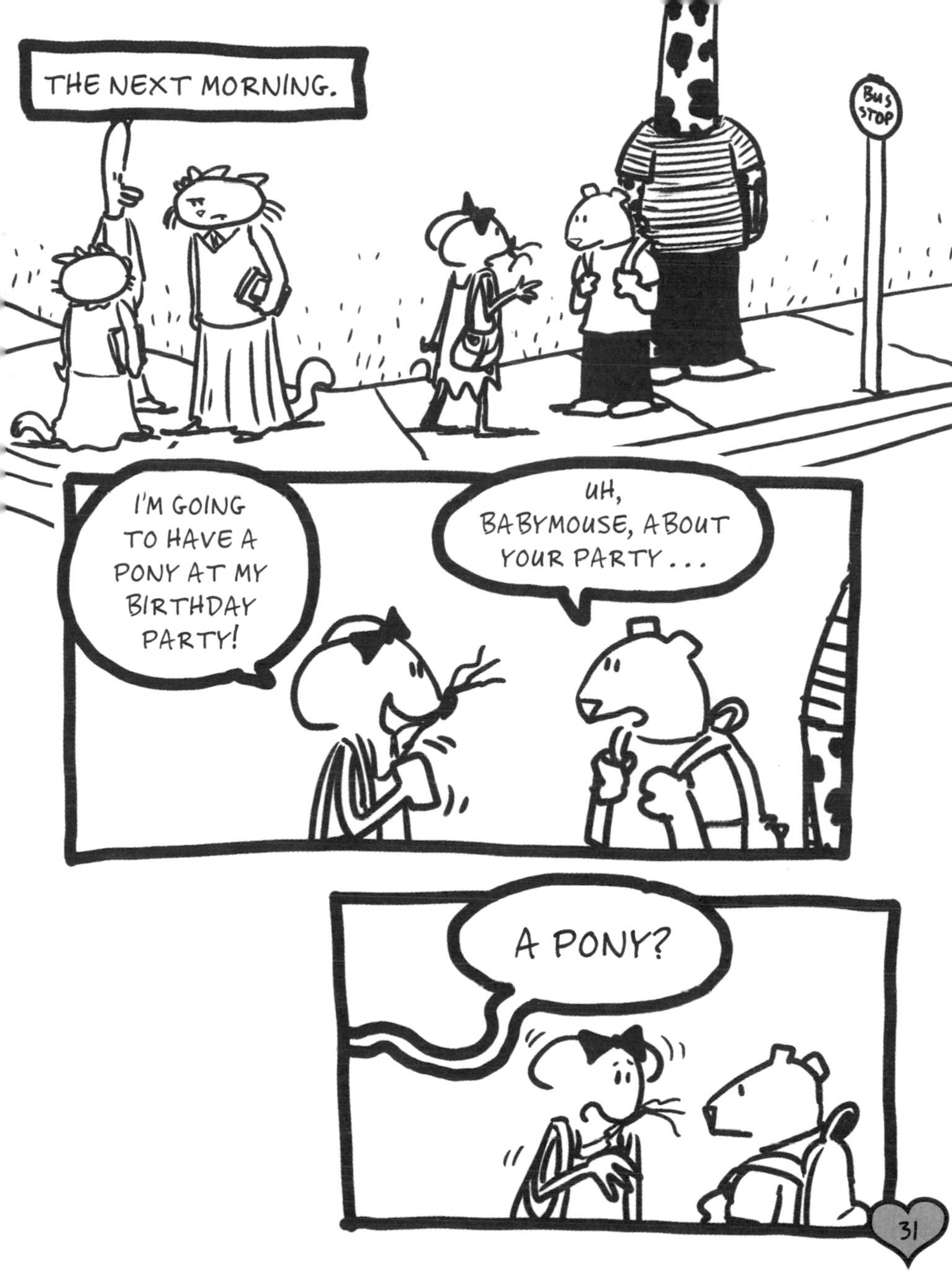
THE NEXT MORNING.
BUS STOP
I'M GOING TO HAVE A PONY AT MY BIRTHDAY PARTY!
UH, BABYMOUSE, ABOUT YOUR PARTY . . .
A PONY?

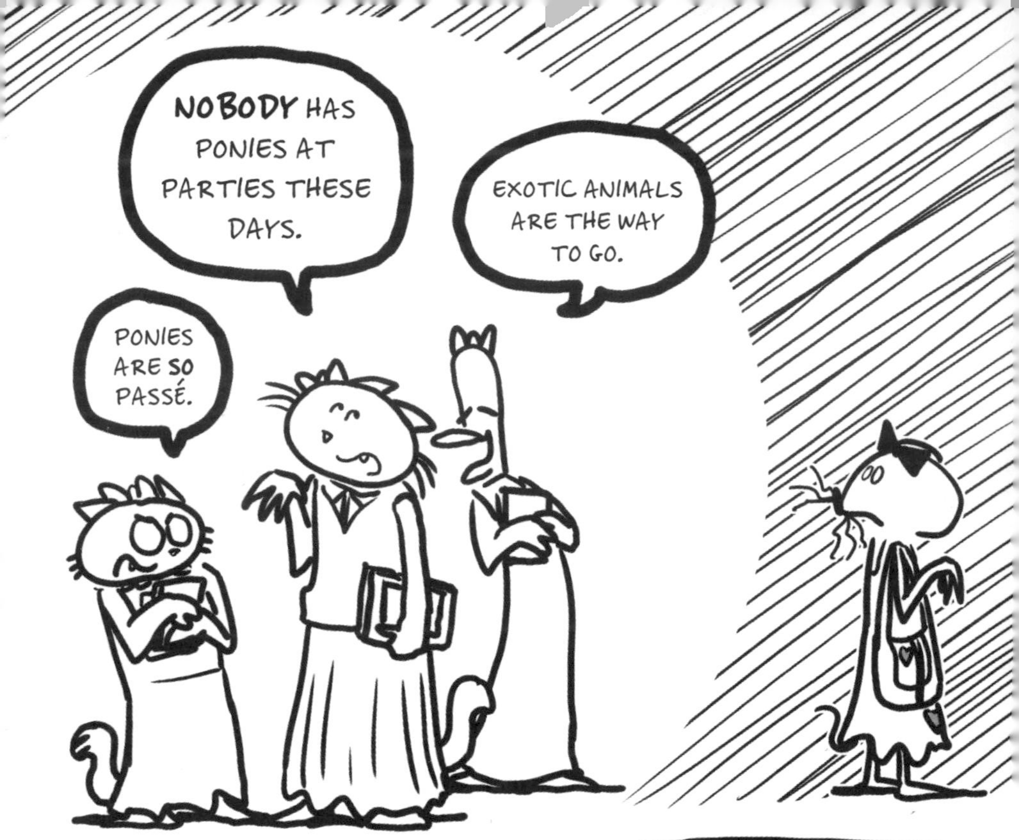
PONIES ARE SO PASSÉ.
NOBODY HAS PONIES AT PARTIES THESE DAYS.
EXOTIC ANIMALS ARE THE WAY TO GO.

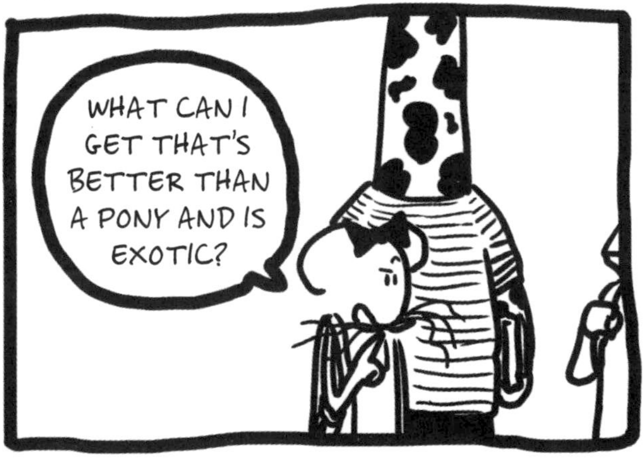
WHAT CAN I GET THAT'S BETTER THAN A PONY AND IS EXOTIC?

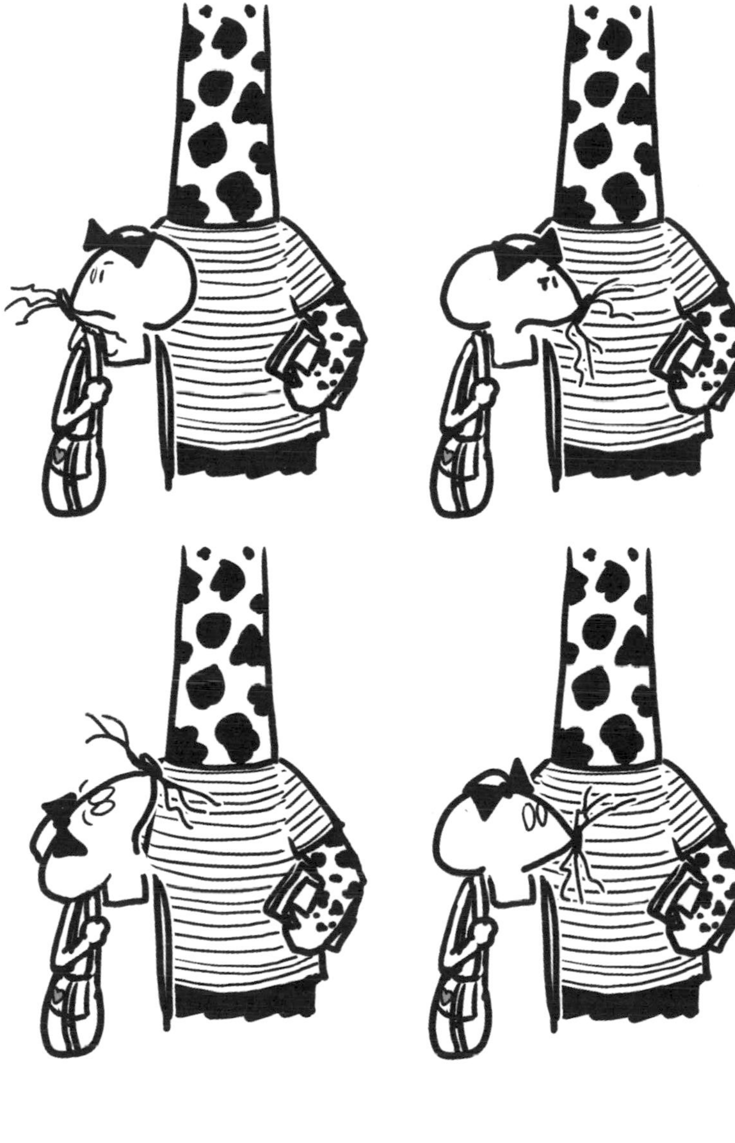

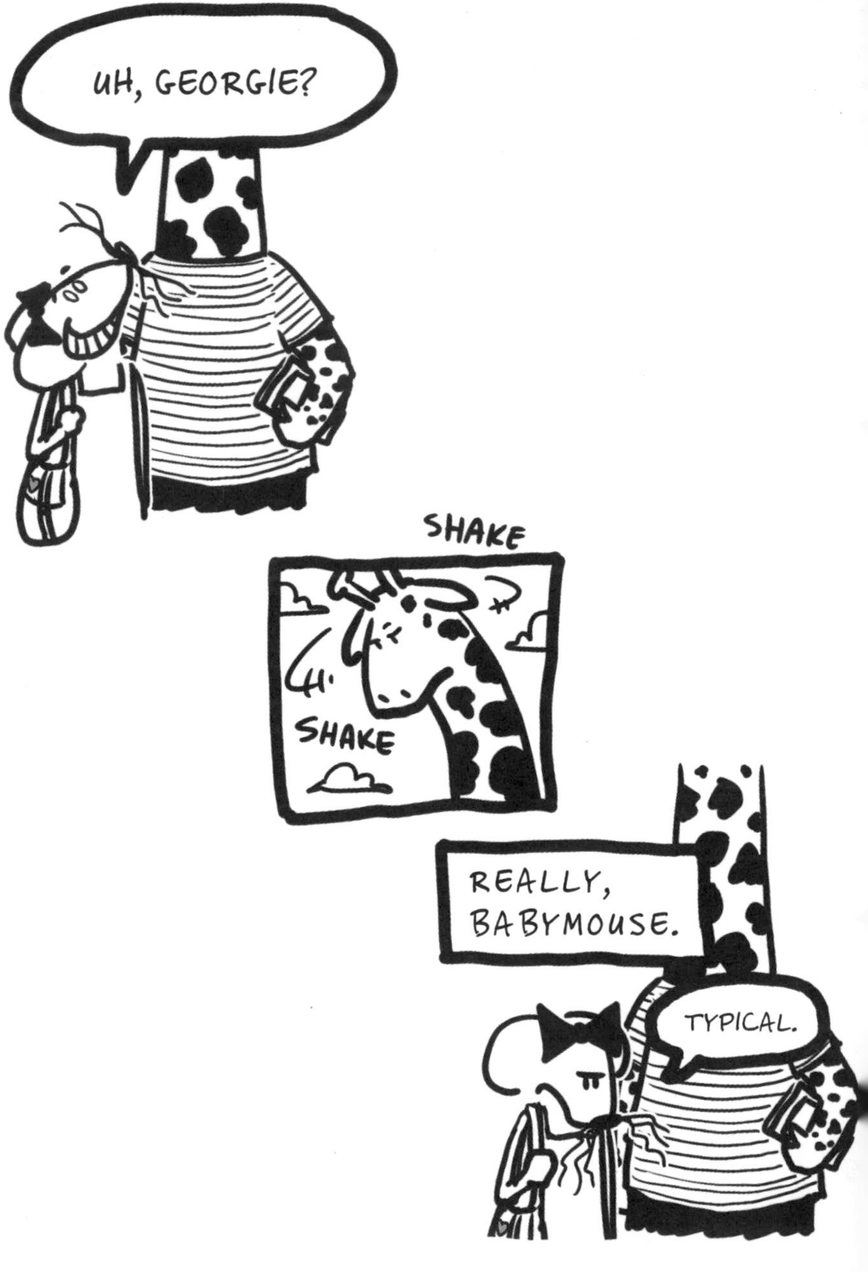
UH, GEORGIE?
SHAKE
SHAKE
REALLY, BABYMOUSE.
TYPICAL.

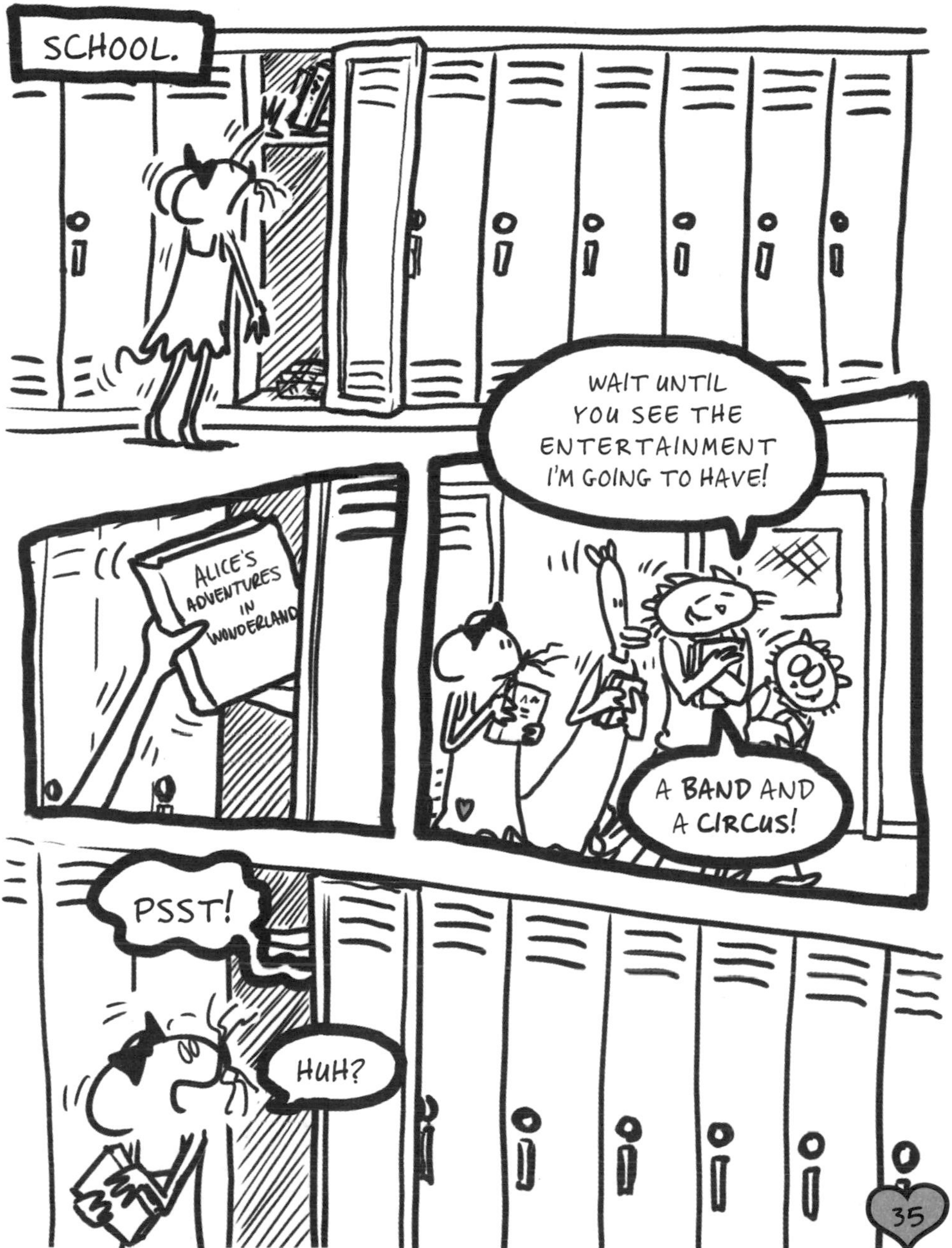
SCHOOL.
ALICE'S ADVENTURES IN WONDERLAND
WAIT UNTIL YOU SEE THE ENTERTAINMENT I'M GOING TO HAVE!
A BAND AND A CIRCUS!
PSST!
HUH?

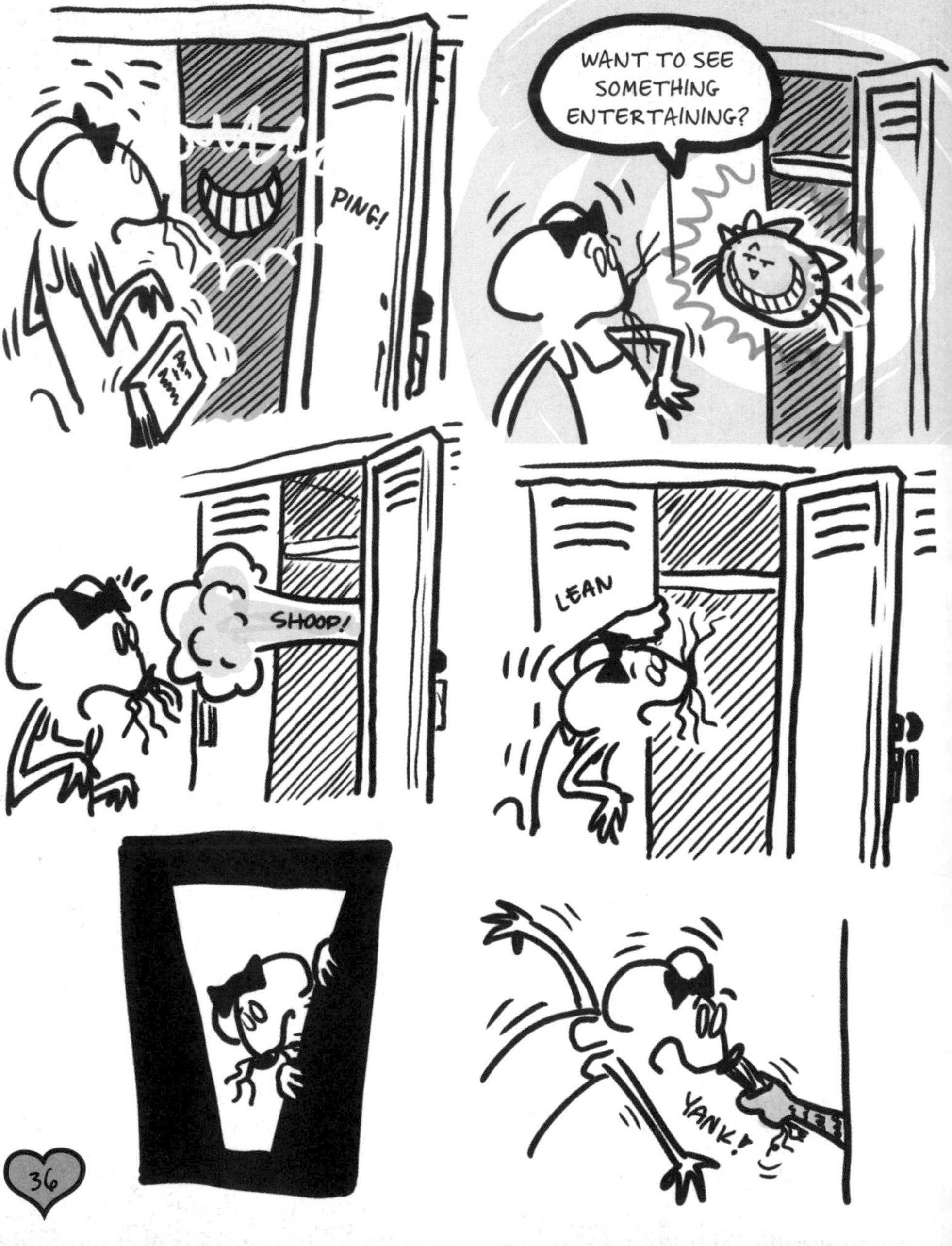
PING!
WANT TO SEE SOMETHING ENTERTAINING?
SHOOP!
LEAN
YANK!

HA!
HEEEYYYYYYY!!!

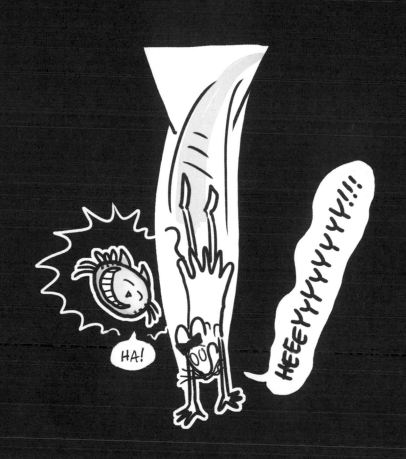

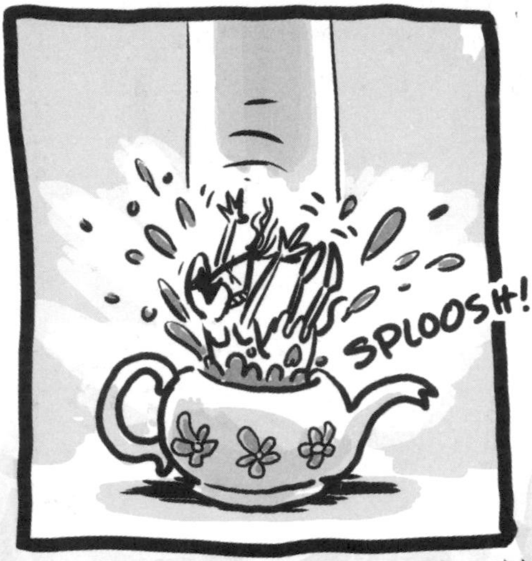
SPLOOSH!

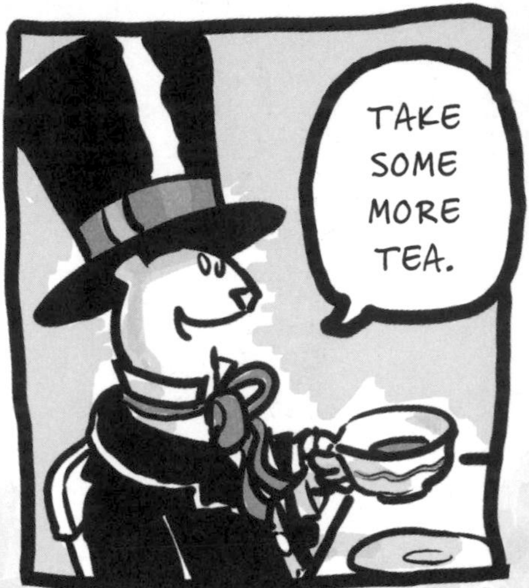
TAKE SOME MORE TEA.

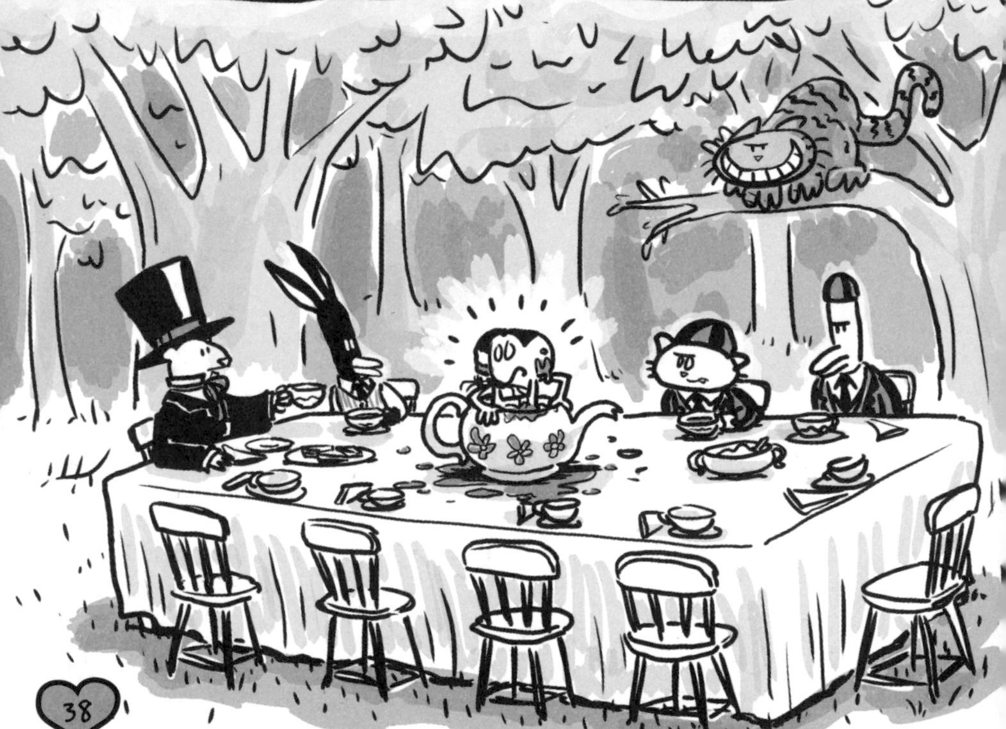

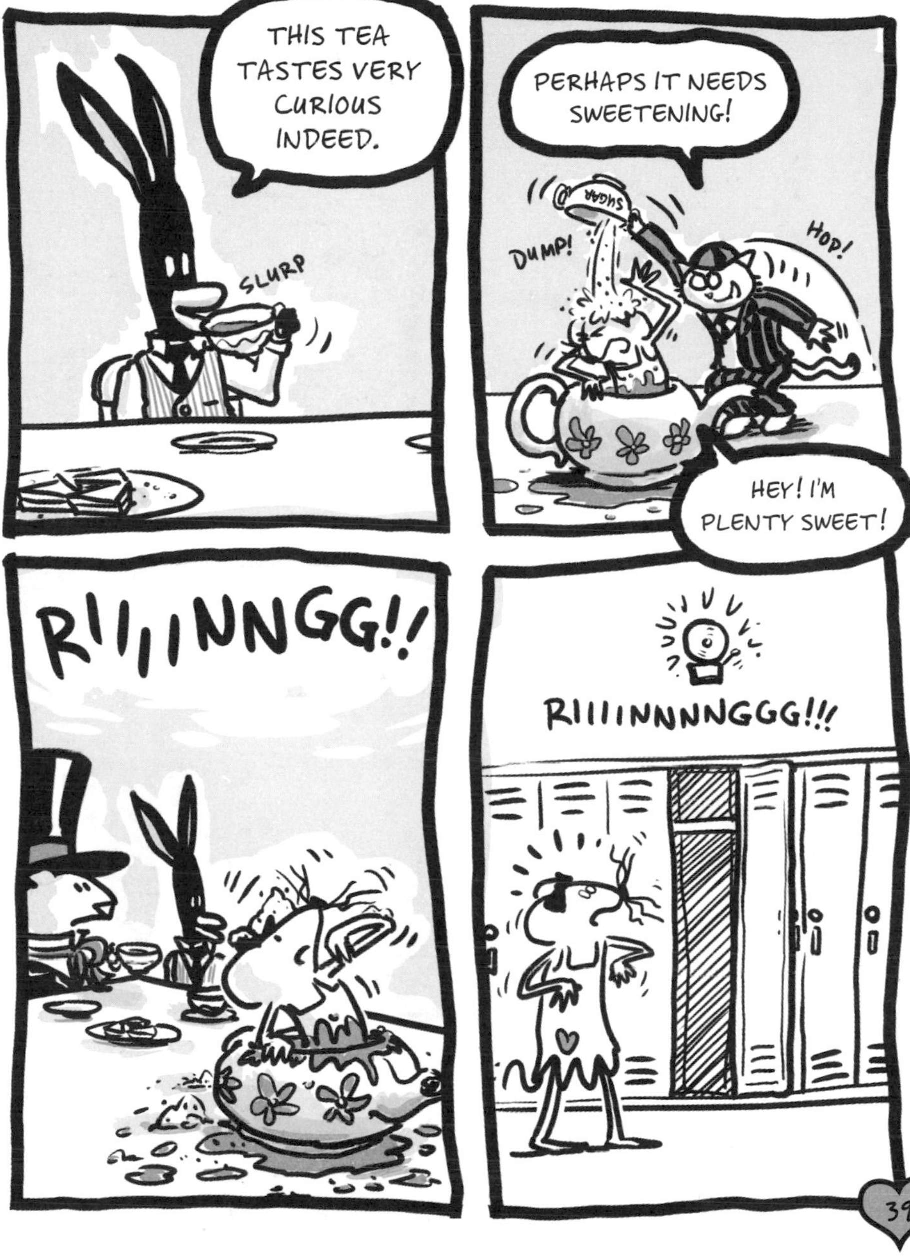

THIS TEA TASTES VERY CURIOUS INDEED.
SLURP
PERHAPS IT NEEDS SWEETENING!
SUGAR
DUMP!
HOP!
HEY! I'M PLENTY SWEET!
RIIIINNGG!!
RIIIINNNNGGG!!!

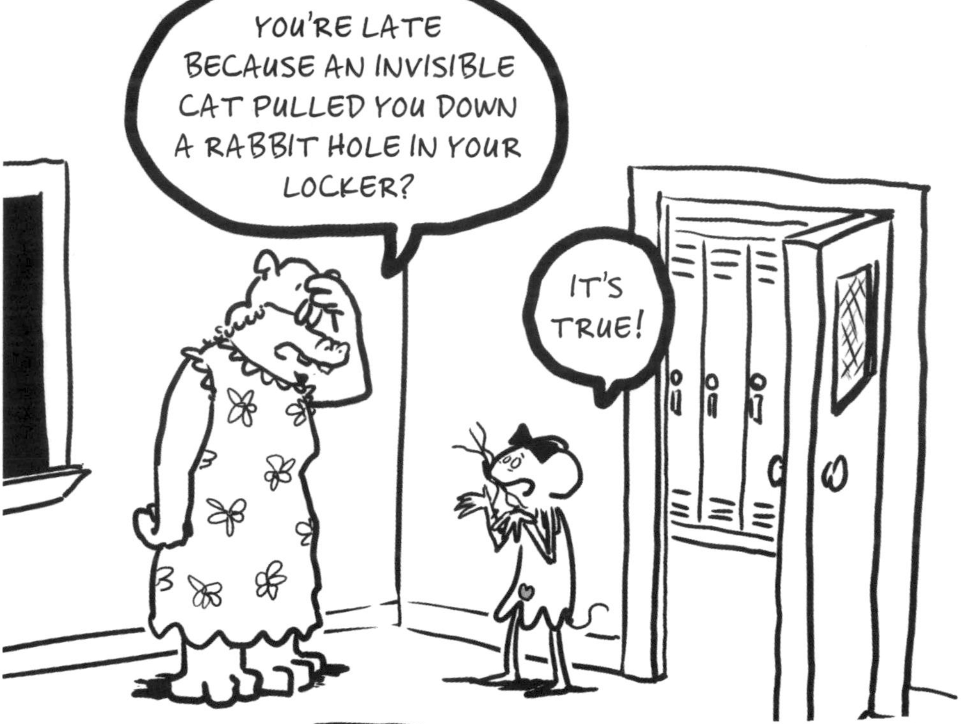
YOU'RE LATE BECAUSE AN INVISIBLE CAT PULLED YOU DOWN A RABBIT HOLE IN YOUR LOCKER?
IT'S TRUE!

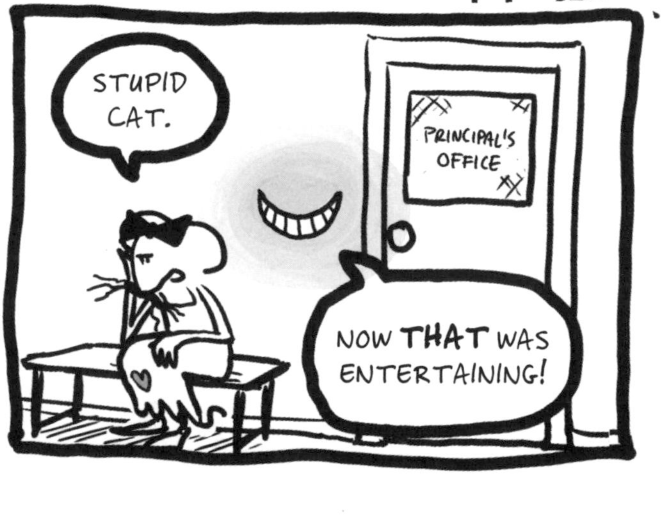
STUPID CAT.
PRINCIPAL'S OFFICE
NOW **THAT** WAS ENTERTAINING!

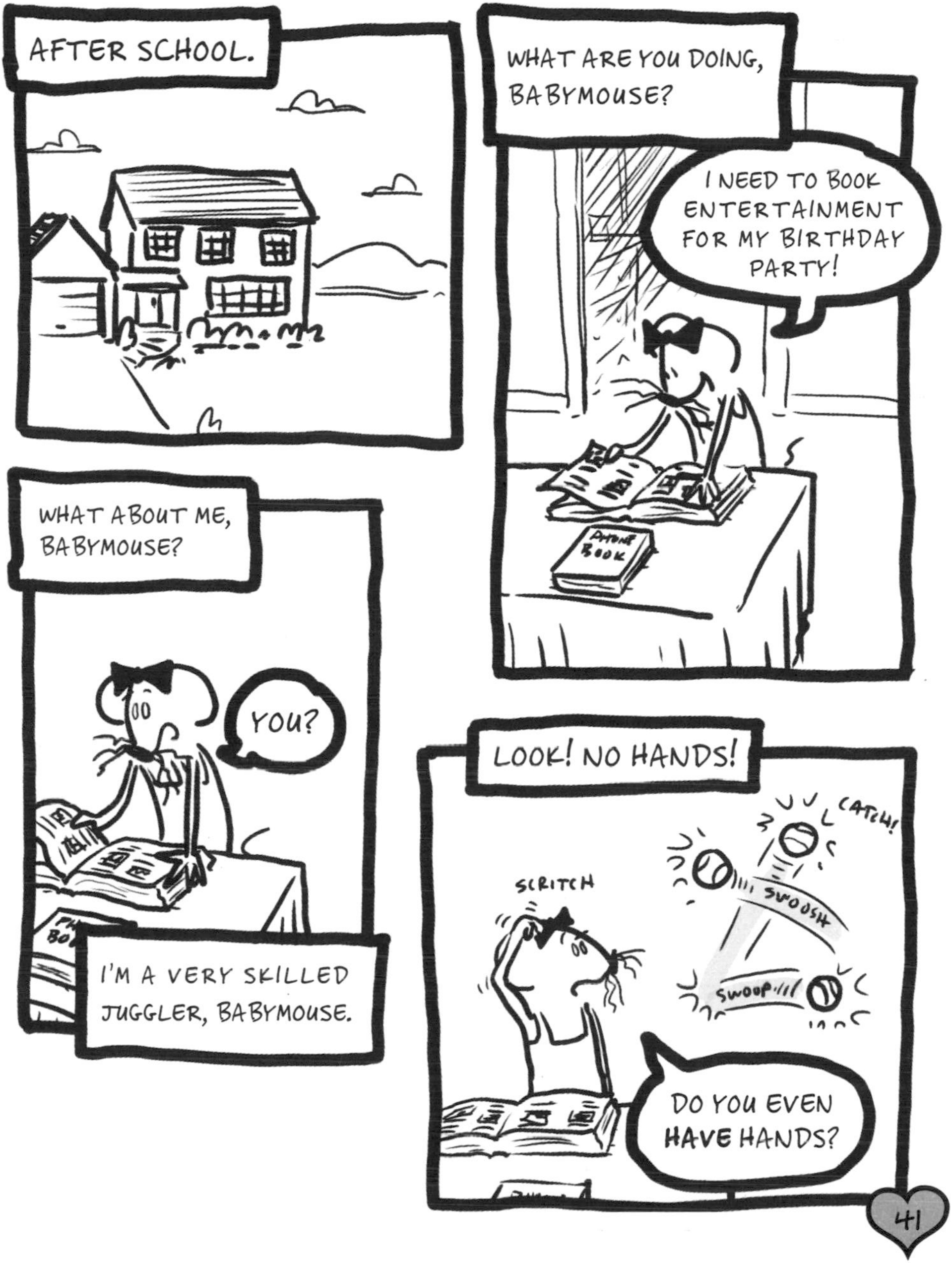
AFTER SCHOOL.
WHAT ARE YOU DOING, BABYMOUSE?
I NEED TO BOOK ENTERTAINMENT FOR MY BIRTHDAY PARTY!
PHONE BOOK
WHAT ABOUT ME, BABYMOUSE?
YOU?
I'M A VERY SKILLED JUGGLER, BABYMOUSE.
LOOK! NO HANDS!
CATCH!
SCRITCH
SWOOSH
SWOOP
DO YOU EVEN HAVE HANDS?

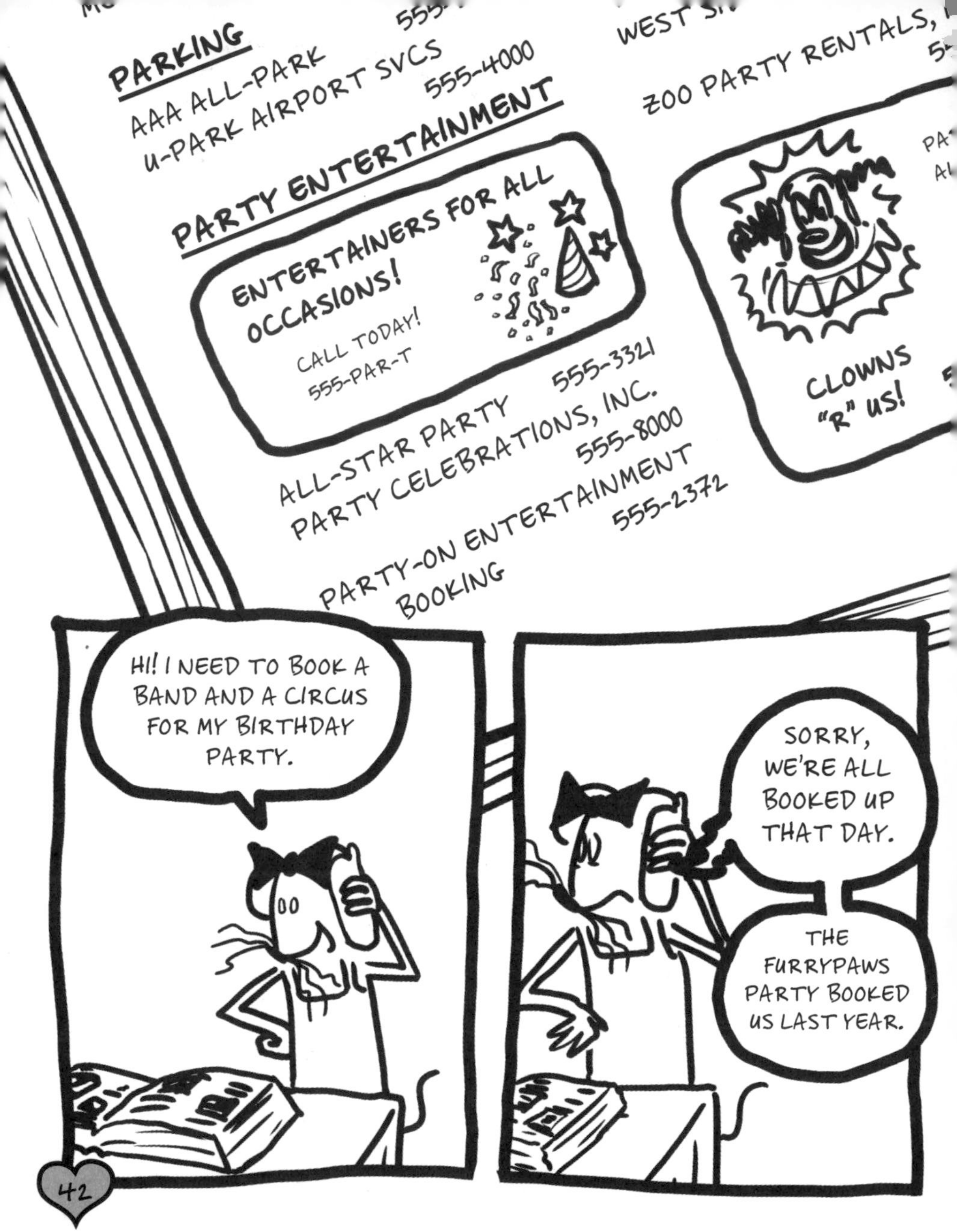
PARKING
AAA ALL-PARK
U-PARK AIRPORT SVCS 555-4000
PARTY ENTERTAINMENT
ENTERTAINERS FOR ALL OCCASIONS!
CALL TODAY! 555-PAR-T
ALL-STAR PARTY 555-3321
PARTY CELEBRATIONS, INC. 555-8000
PARTY-ON ENTERTAINMENT 555-2372
BOOKING
WEST
ZOO PARTY RENTALS,
CLOWNS "R" US!
HI! I NEED TO BOOK A BAND AND A CIRCUS FOR MY BIRTHDAY PARTY.
SORRY, WE'RE ALL BOOKED UP THAT DAY.
THE FURRYPAWS PARTY BOOKED US LAST YEAR.

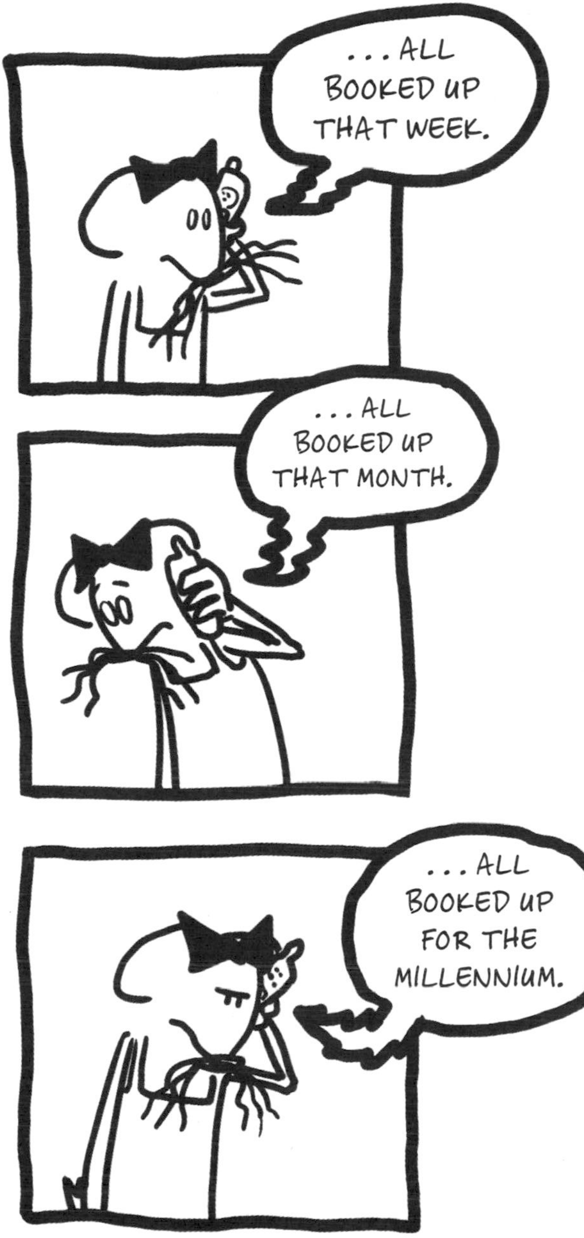
. . . ALL BOOKED UP THAT WEEK.
. . . ALL BOOKED UP THAT MONTH.
. . . ALL BOOKED UP FOR THE MILLENNIUM.

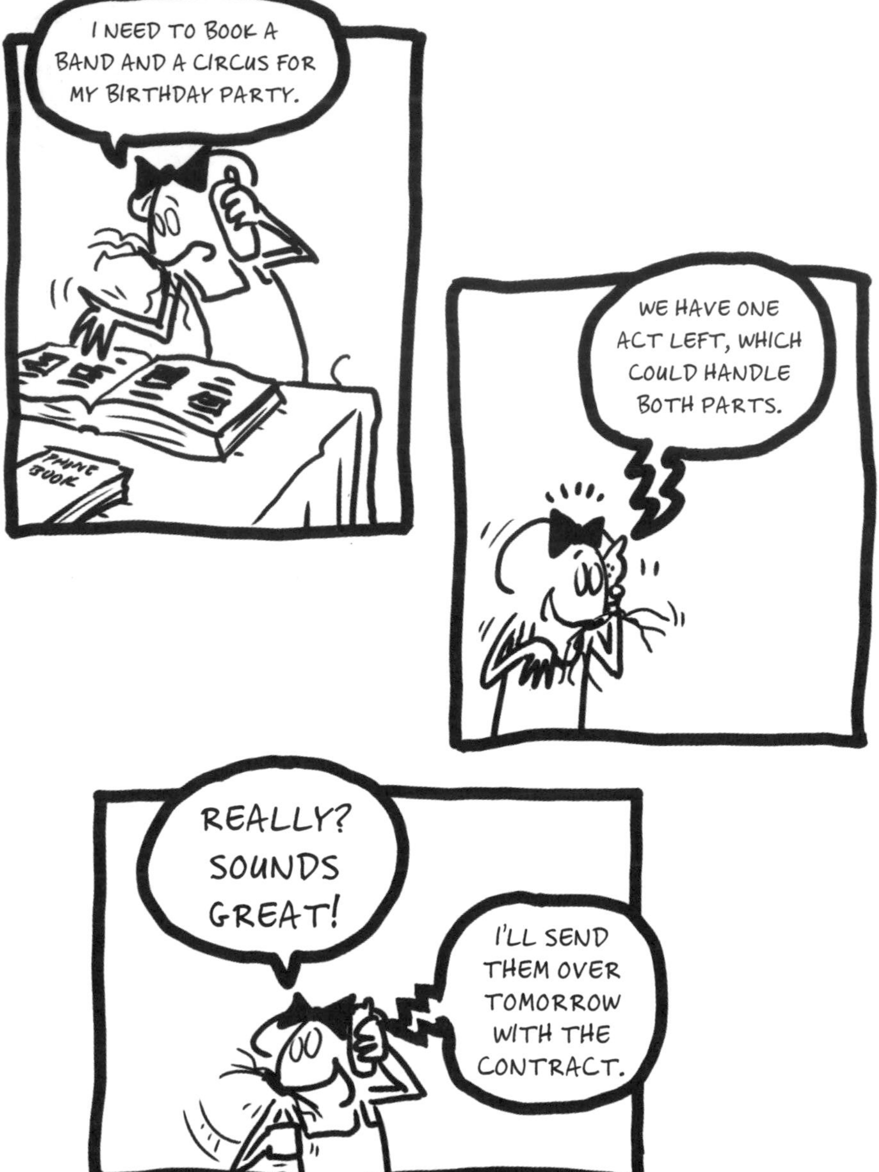
I NEED TO BOOK A BAND AND A CIRCUS FOR MY BIRTHDAY PARTY.
PHONE BOOK
WE HAVE ONE ACT LEFT, WHICH COULD HANDLE BOTH PARTS.
REALLY? SOUNDS GREAT!
I'LL SEND THEM OVER TOMORROW WITH THE CONTRACT.

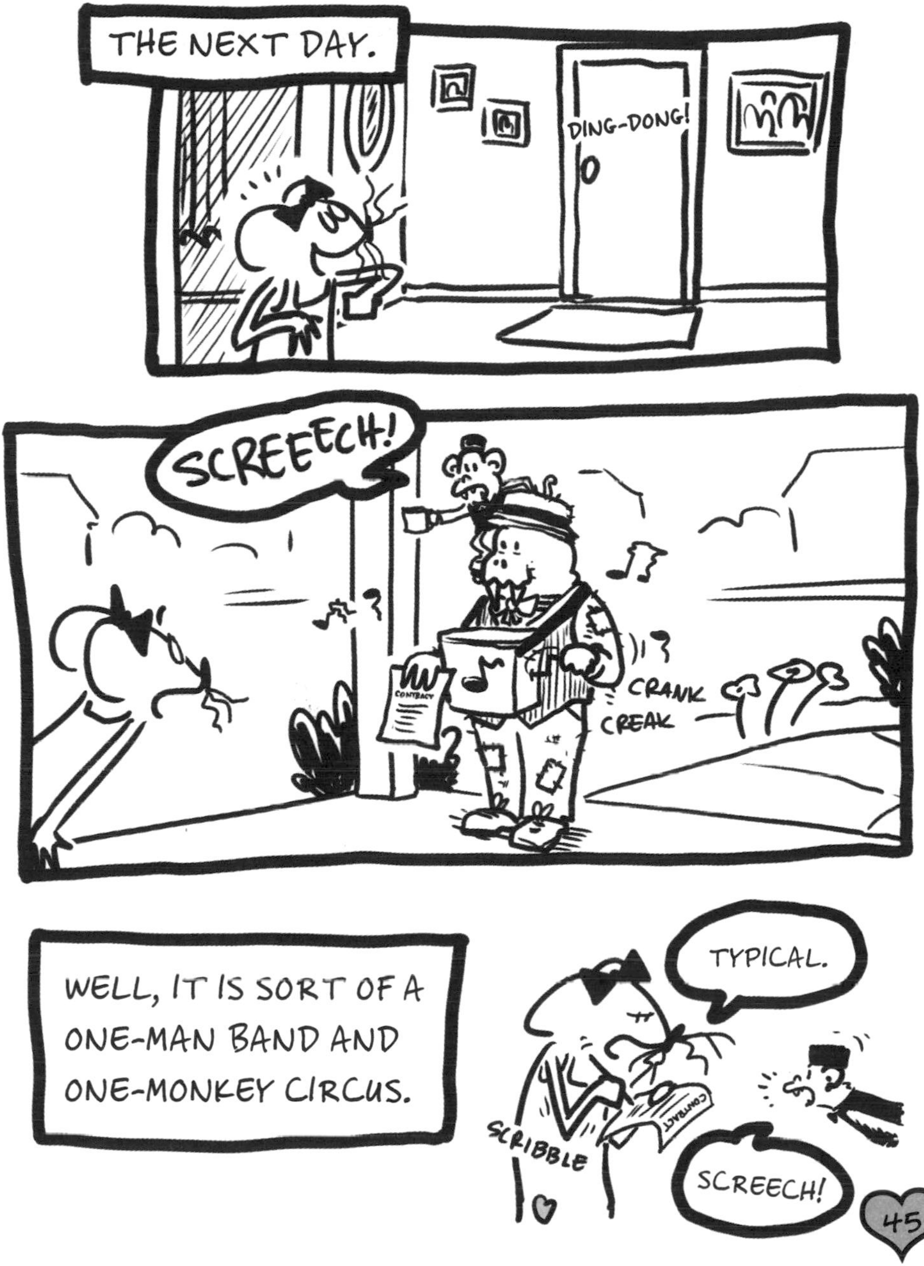
THE NEXT DAY.
DING-DONG!
SCREEECH!
CRANK
CREAK
WELL, IT IS SORT OF A ONE-MAN BAND AND ONE-MONKEY CIRCUS.
TYPICAL.
SCRIBBLE
CONTRACT
SCREECH!

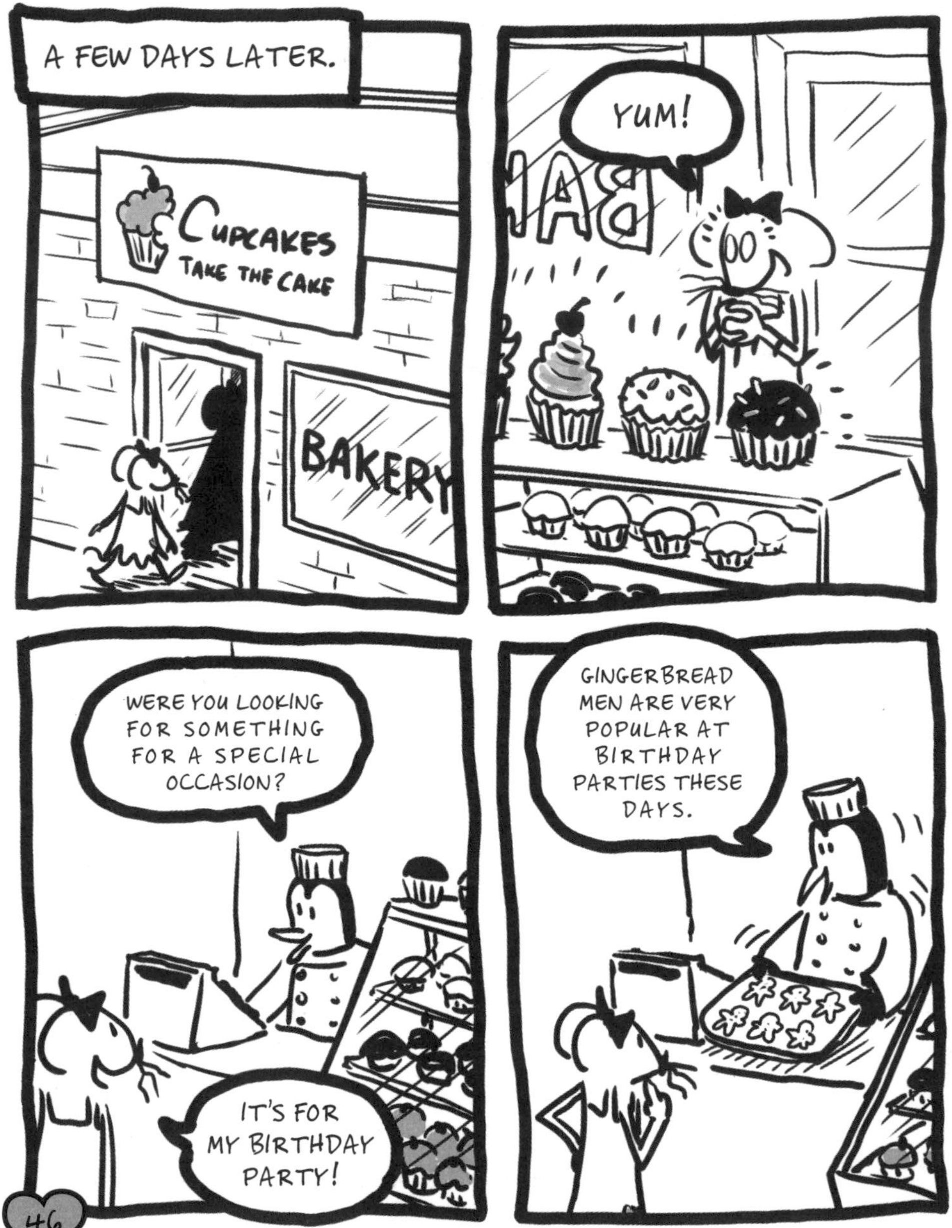
A FEW DAYS LATER.
CUPCAKES TAKE THE CAKE
BAKERY
YUM!
WERE YOU LOOKING FOR SOMETHING FOR A SPECIAL OCCASION?
IT'S FOR MY BIRTHDAY PARTY!
GINGERBREAD MEN ARE VERY POPULAR AT BIRTHDAY PARTIES THESE DAYS.

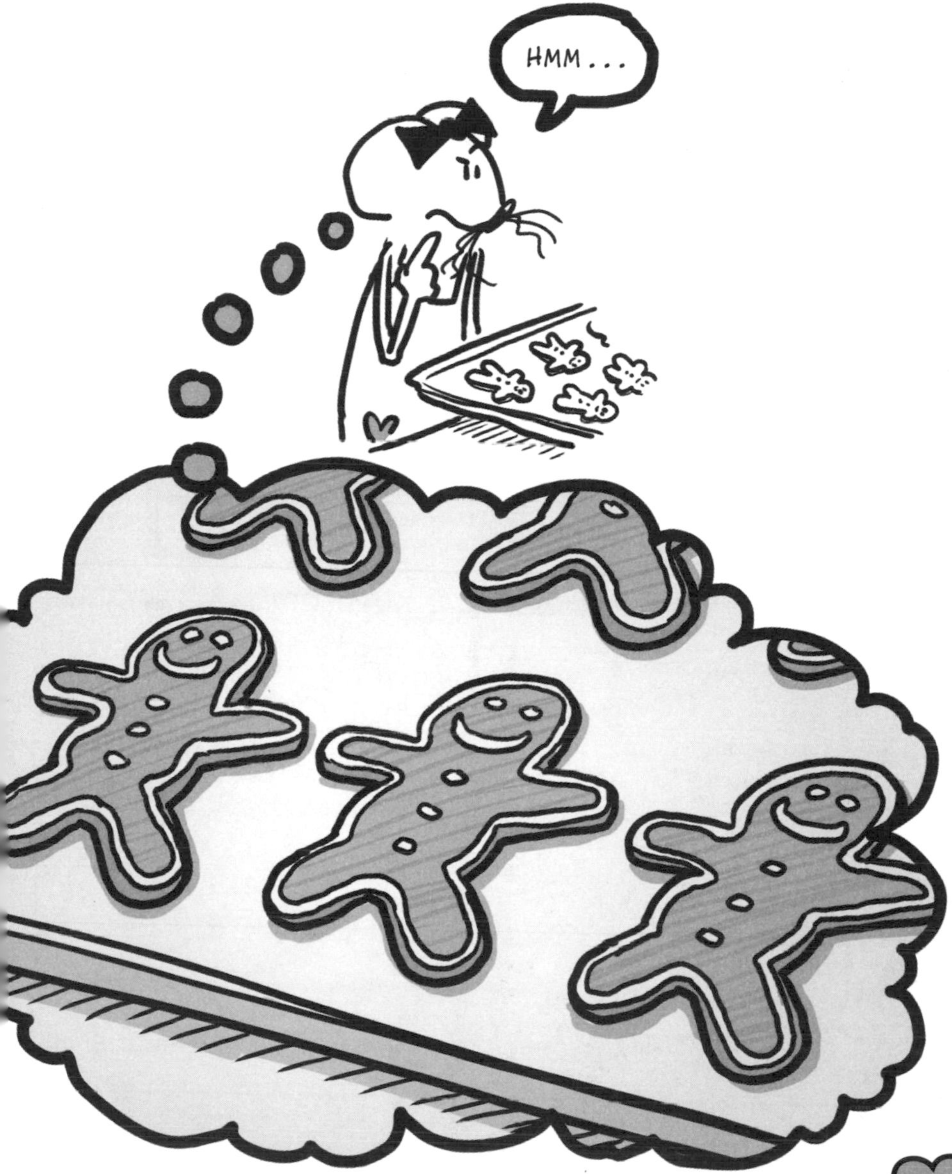
HMM...

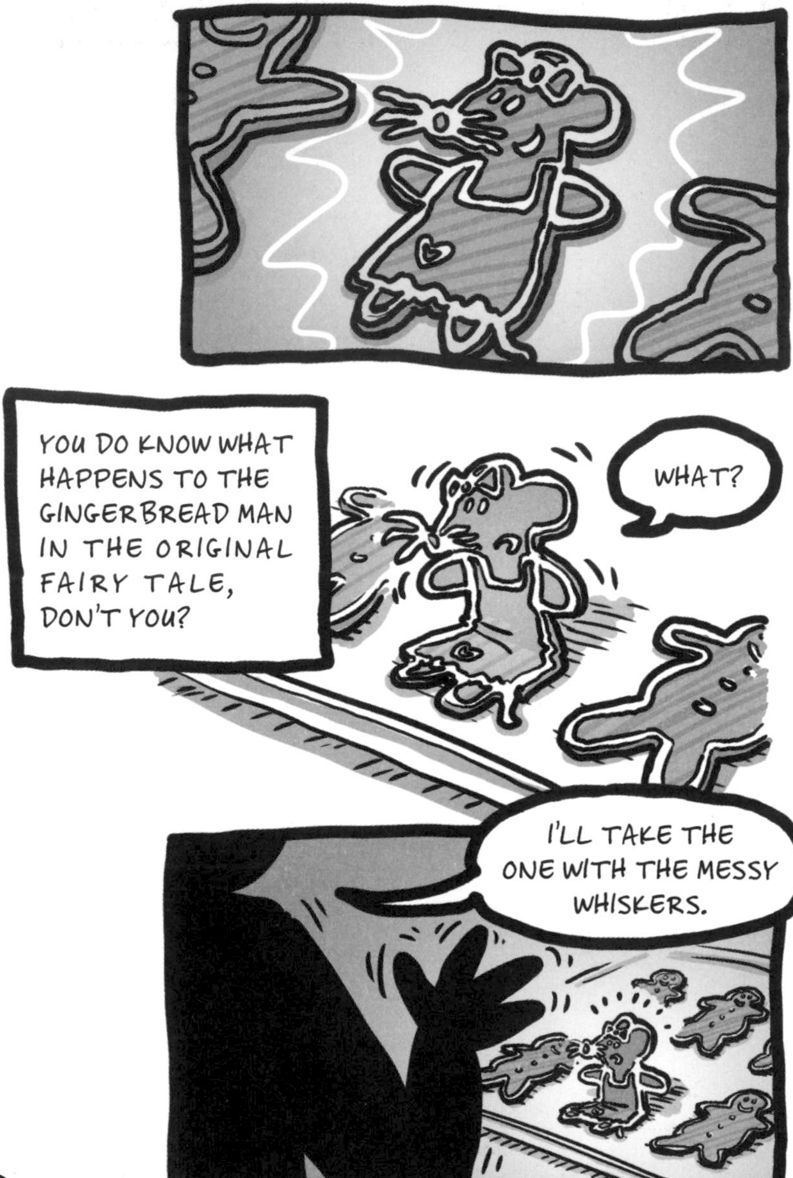
YOU DO KNOW WHAT HAPPENS TO THE GINGERBREAD MAN IN THE ORIGINAL FAIRY TALE, DON'T YOU?
WHAT?
I'LL TAKE THE ONE WITH THE MESSY WHISKERS.

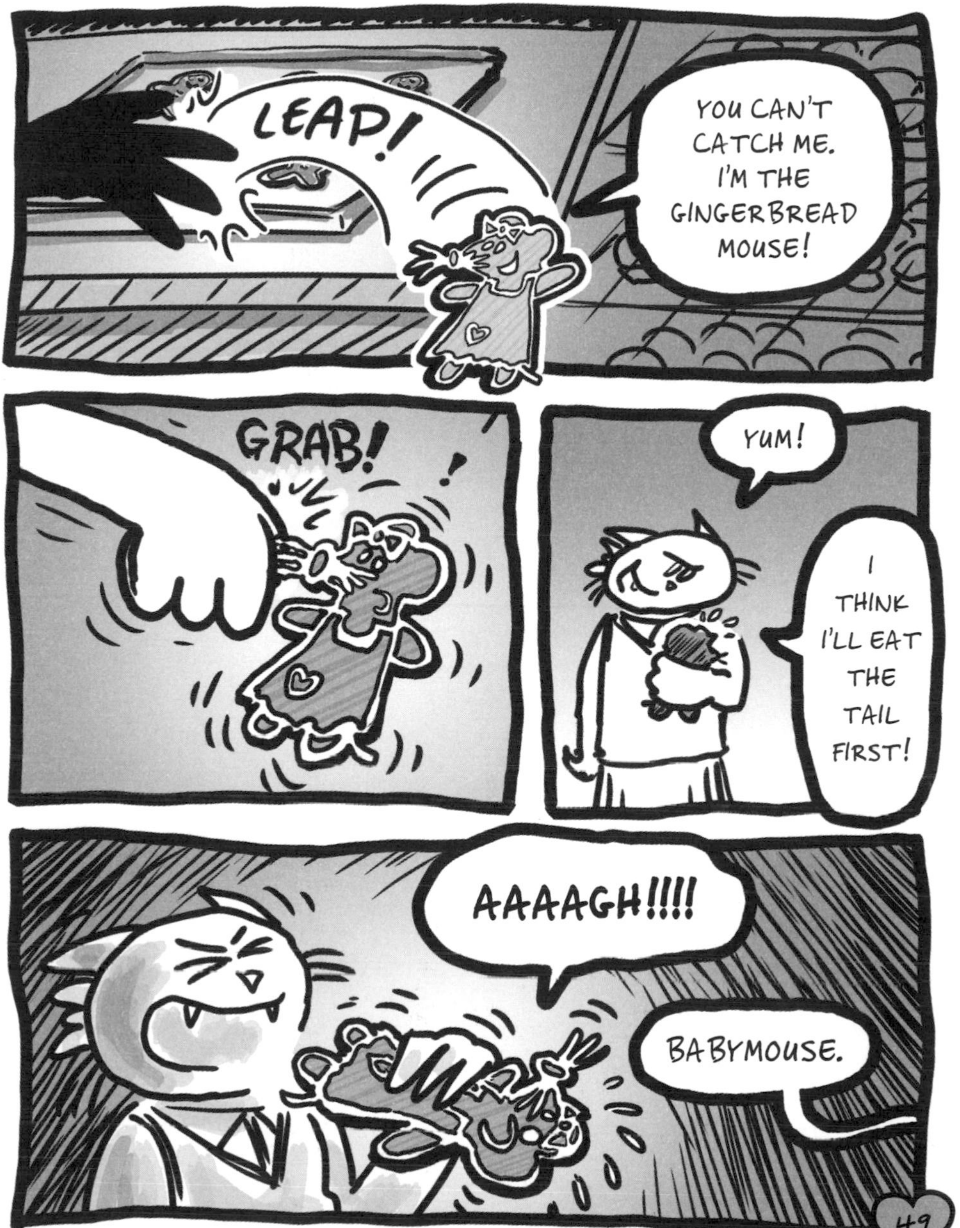
LEAP!
YOU CAN'T CATCH ME. I'M THE GINGERBREAD MOUSE!
GRAB!
!
YUM!
I THINK I'LL EAT THE TAIL FIRST!
AAAAGH!!!!!
BABYMOUSE.

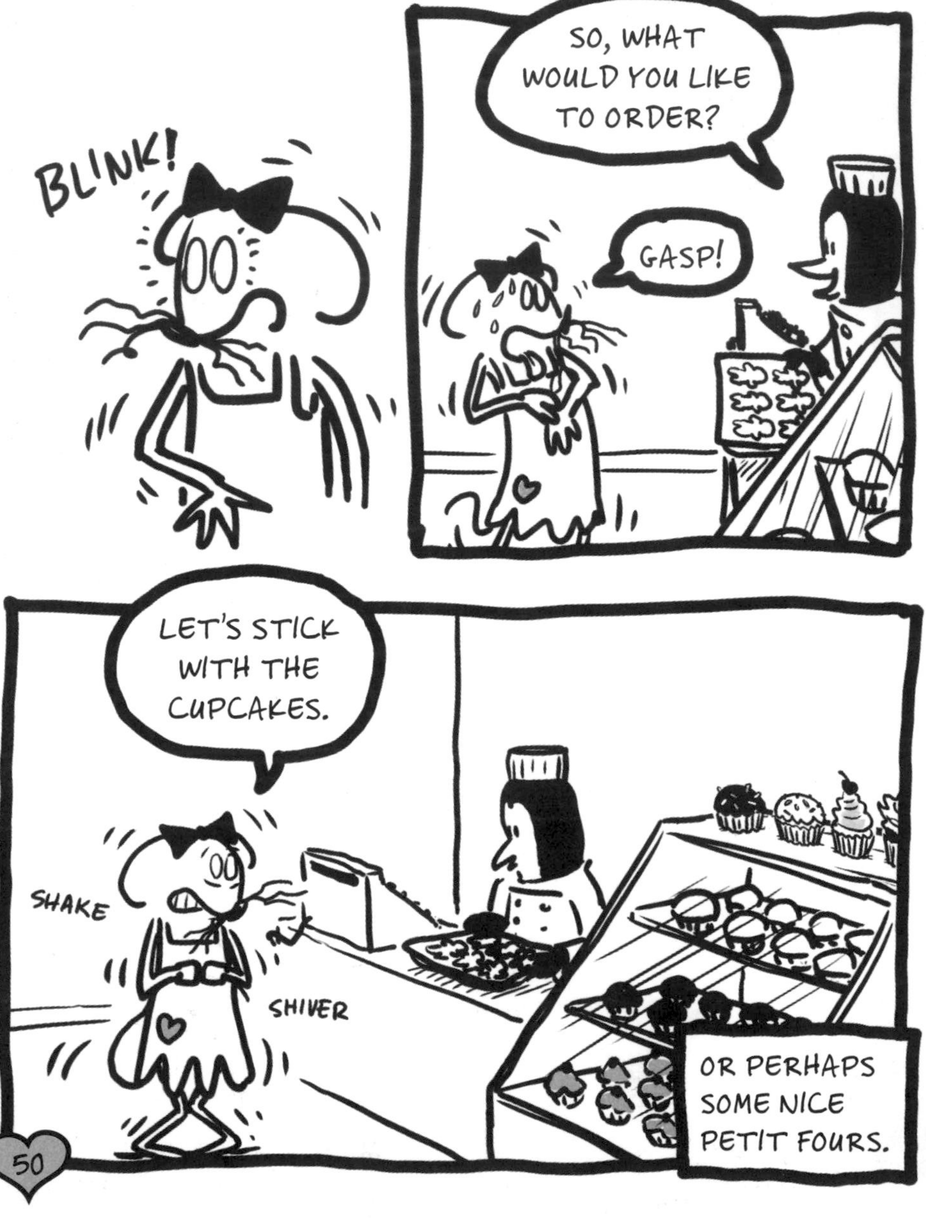
BLINK!
SO, WHAT WOULD YOU LIKE TO ORDER?
GASP!
LET'S STICK WITH THE CUPCAKES.
SHAKE
SHIVER
OR PERHAPS SOME NICE PETIT FOURS.

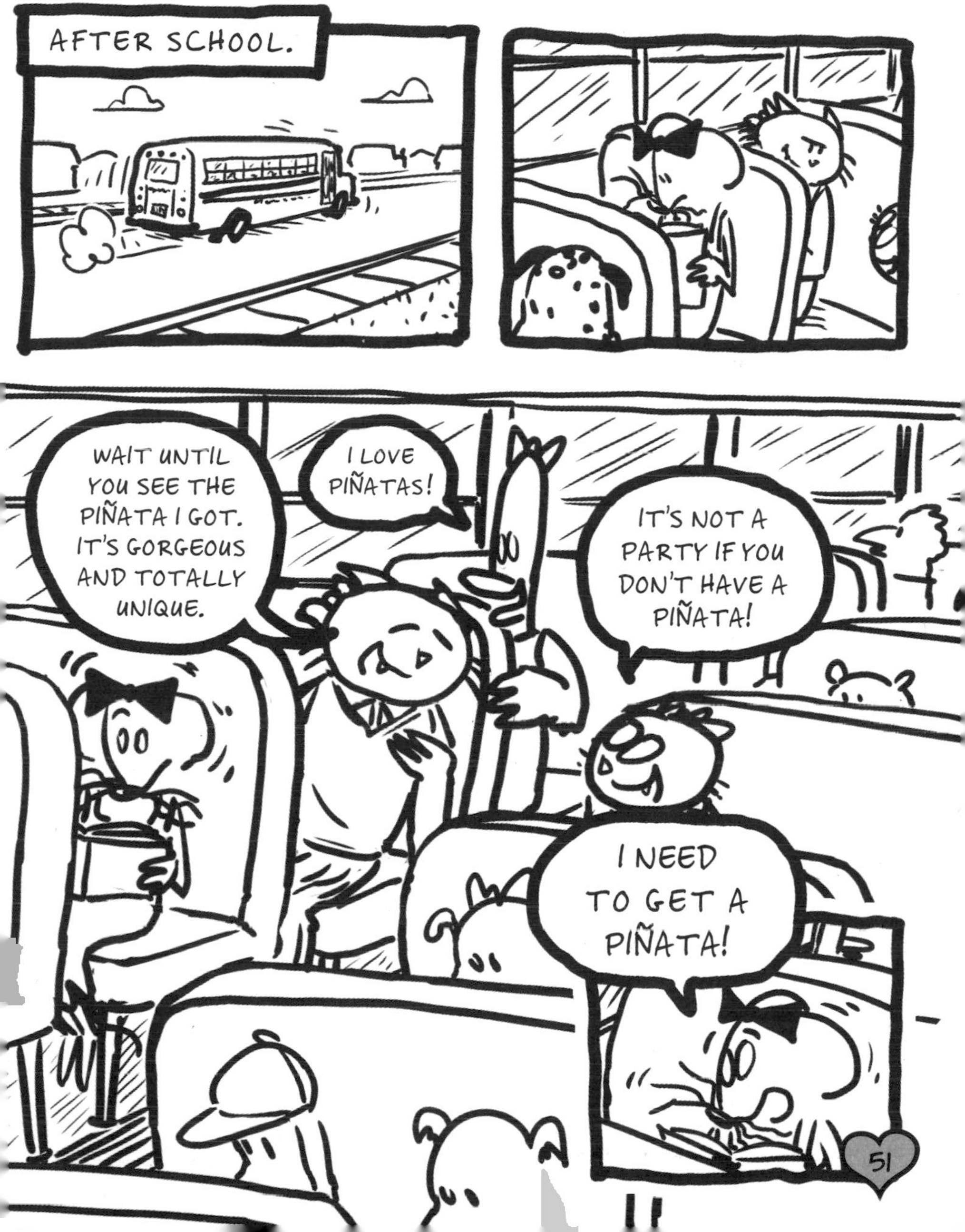
AFTER SCHOOL.
WAIT UNTIL YOU SEE THE PIÑATA I GOT. IT'S GORGEOUS AND TOTALLY UNIQUE.
I LOVE PIÑATAS!
IT'S NOT A PARTY IF YOU DON'T HAVE A PIÑATA!
I NEED TO GET A PIÑATA!

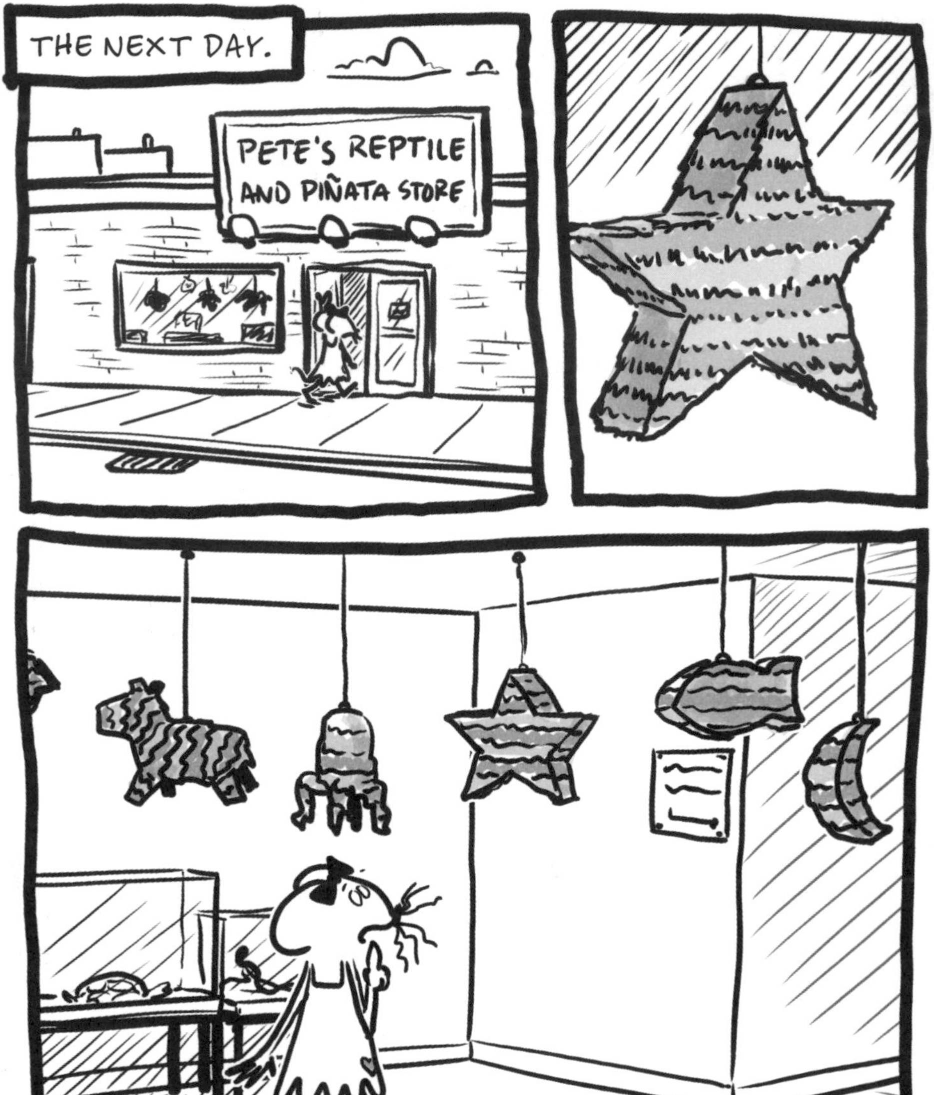

THE NEXT DAY.
PETE'S REPTILE AND PIÑATA STORE

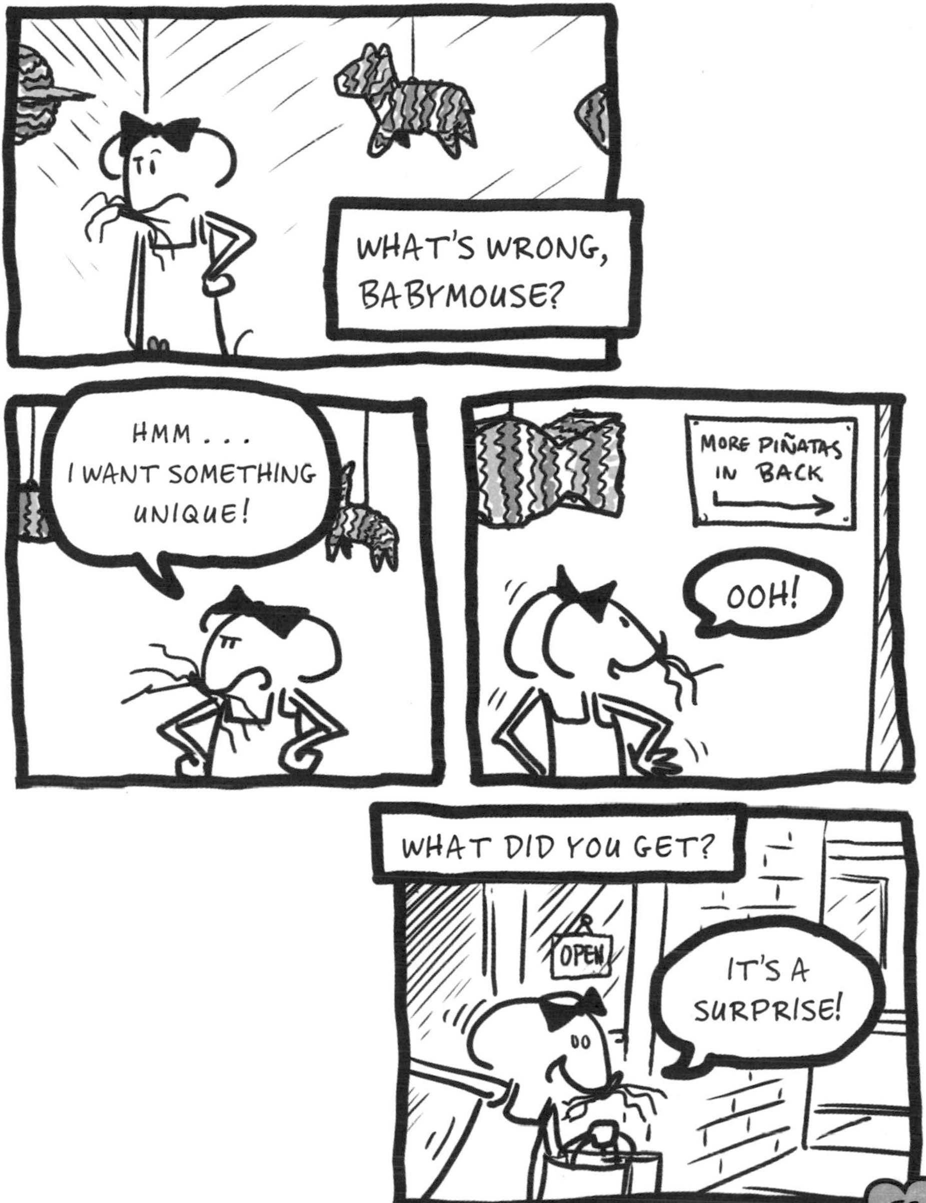
WHAT'S WRONG, BABYMOUSE?
HMM . . . I WANT SOMETHING UNIQUE!
MORE PIÑATAS IN BACK
OOH!
WHAT DID YOU GET?
OPEN
IT'S A SURPRISE!

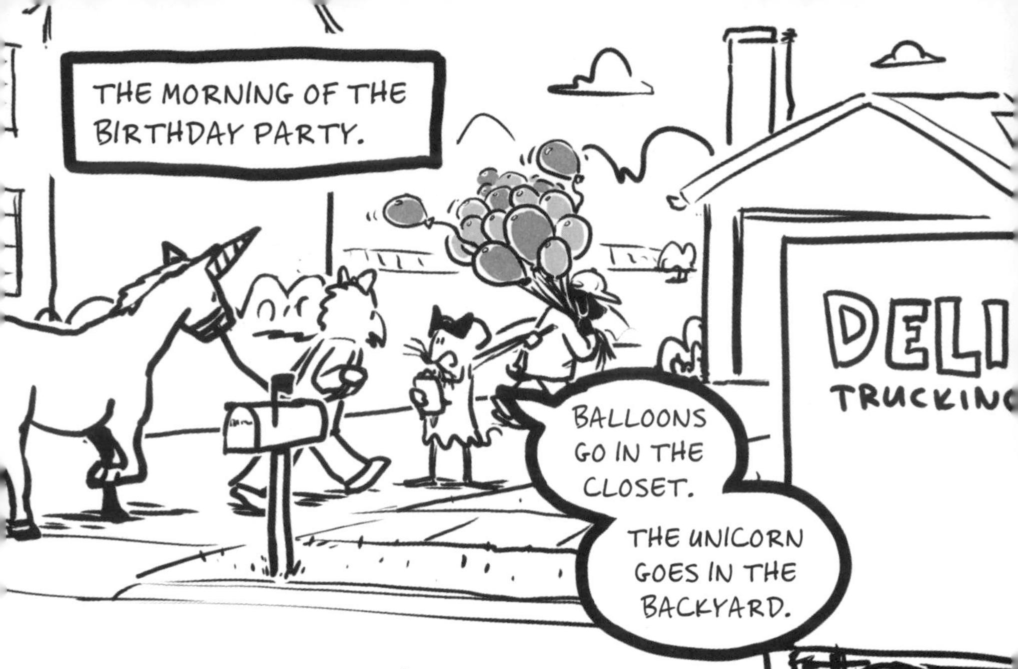
THE MORNING OF THE BIRTHDAY PARTY.
BALLOONS GO IN THE CLOSET.
THE UNICORN GOES IN THE BACKYARD.
DELI
TRUCKIN

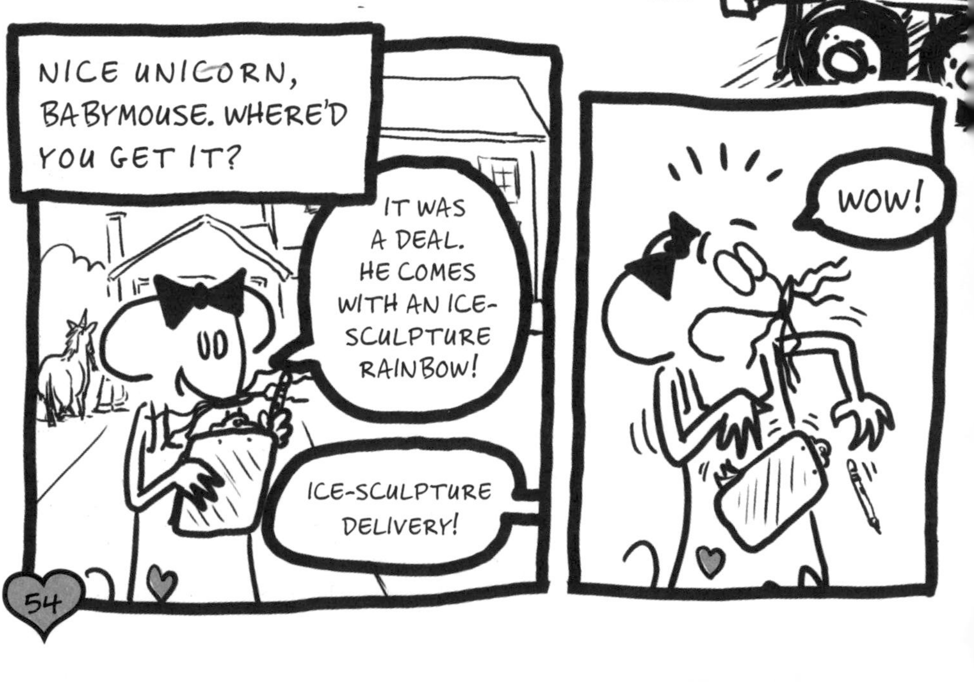
NICE UNICORN, BABYMOUSE. WHERE'D YOU GET IT?
IT WAS A DEAL. HE COMES WITH AN ICE-SCULPTURE RAINBOW!
ICE-SCULPTURE DELIVERY!
WOW!

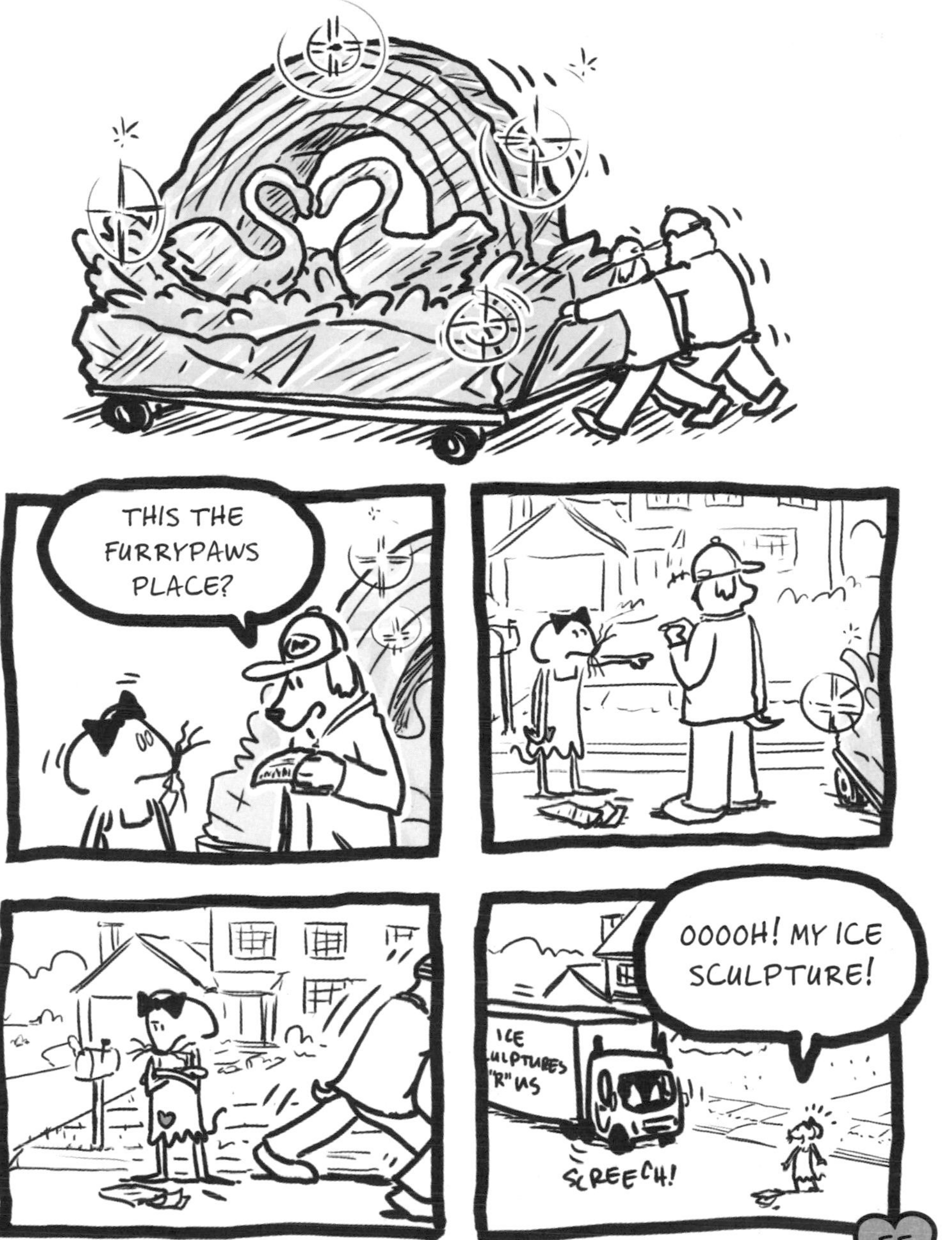
THIS THE FURRYPAWS PLACE?
ICE SCULPTURES "R" US
SCREECH!
OOOOH! MY ICE SCULPTURE!

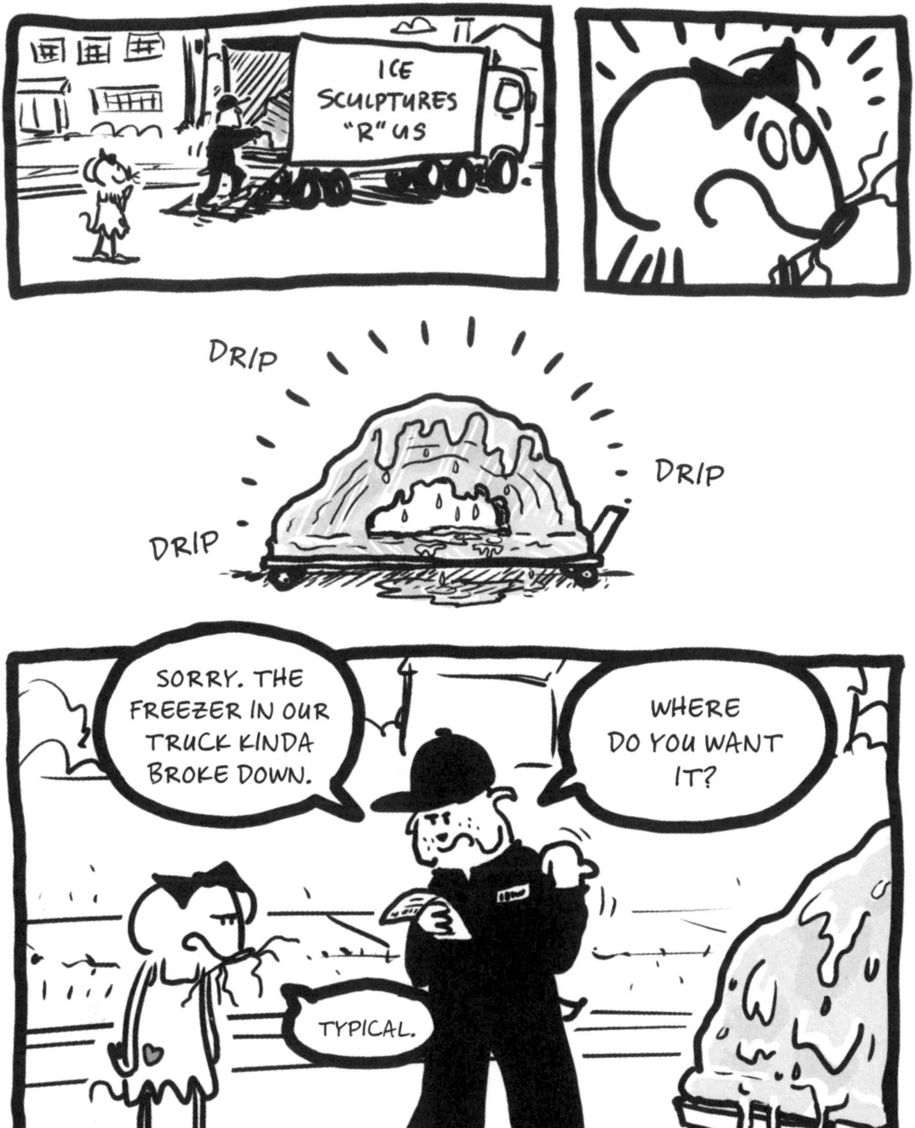

ICE SCULPTURES "R" US
DRIP
DRIP
DRIP
SORRY. THE FREEZER IN OUR TRUCK KINDA BROKE DOWN.
WHERE DO YOU WANT IT?
TYPICAL.

A LITTLE LATER.

MOM, THE CUPCAKES HAVEN'T ARRIVED.

LET ME CALL THE BAKERY.

BABYMOUSE, THE BAKER CAN'T FIND YOUR ORDER.

HE SWORE HE MADE THEM, BUT WHEN HE WENT IN THIS MORNING, THEY WERE MISSING.

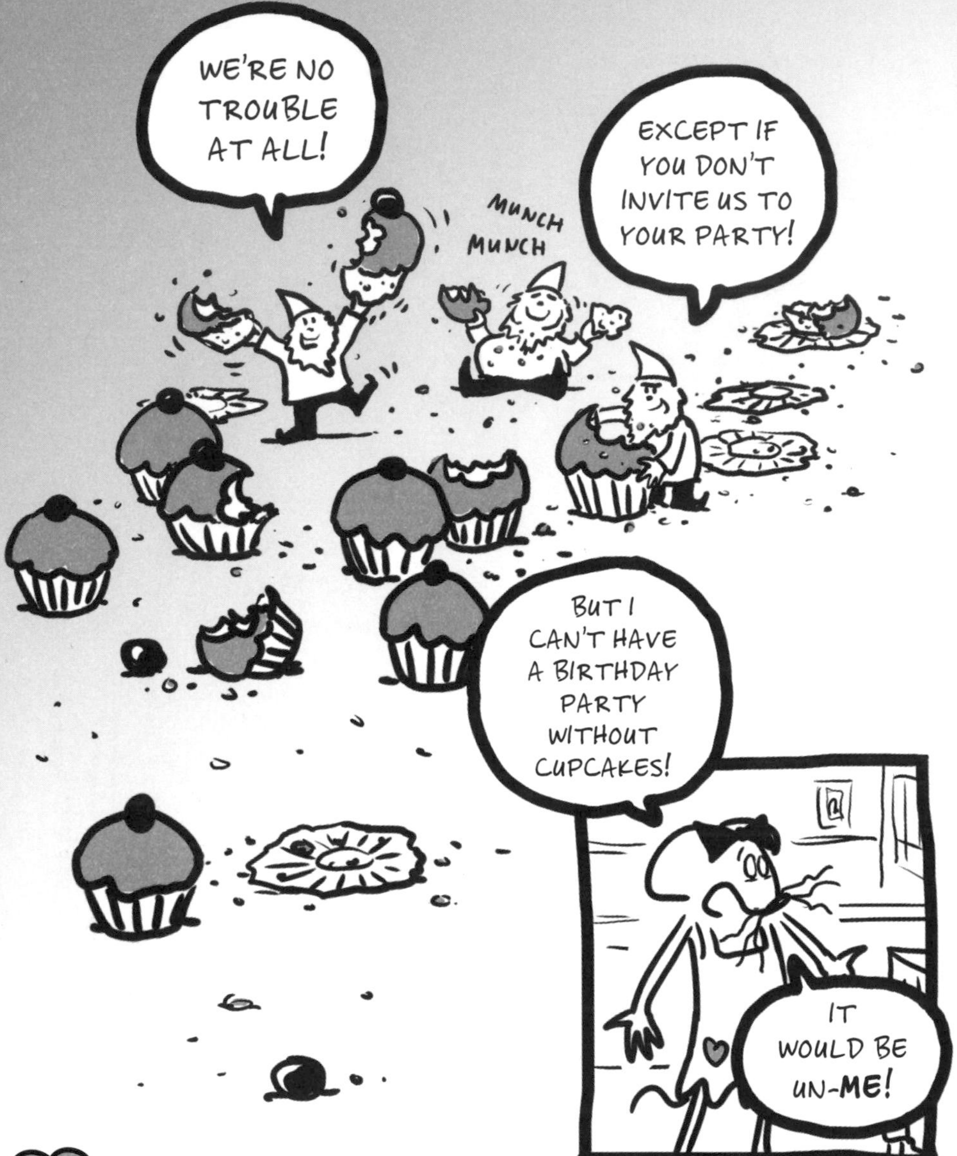
WE'RE NO TROUBLE AT ALL!
MUNCH
MUNCH
EXCEPT IF YOU DON'T INVITE US TO YOUR PARTY!
BUT I CAN'T HAVE A BIRTHDAY PARTY WITHOUT CUPCAKES!
IT WOULD BE UN-ME!

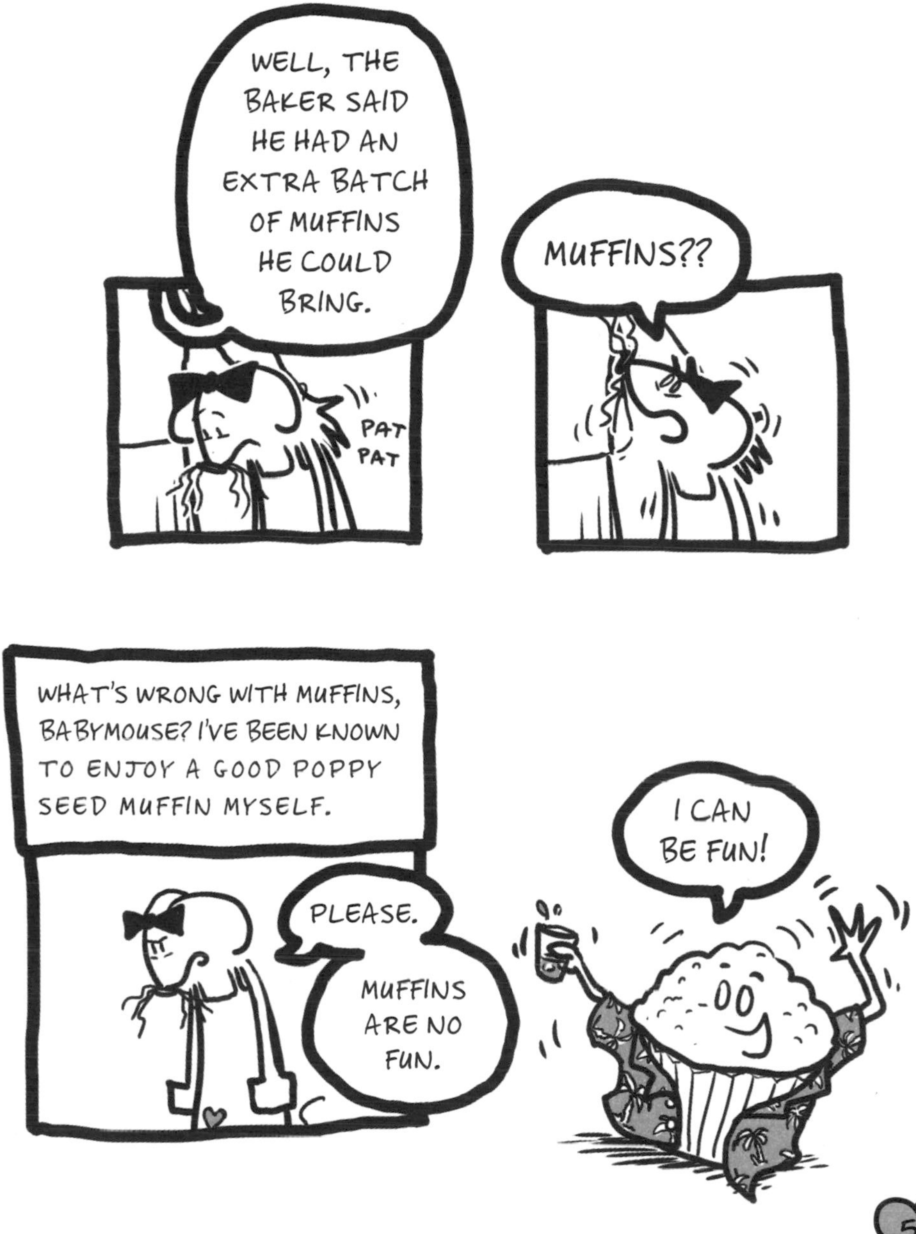
WELL, THE BAKER SAID HE HAD AN EXTRA BATCH OF MUFFINS HE COULD BRING.
PAT PAT
MUFFINS??
WHAT'S WRONG WITH MUFFINS, BABYMOUSE? I'VE BEEN KNOWN TO ENJOY A GOOD POPPY SEED MUFFIN MYSELF.
PLEASE.
MUFFINS ARE NO FUN.
I CAN BE FUN!

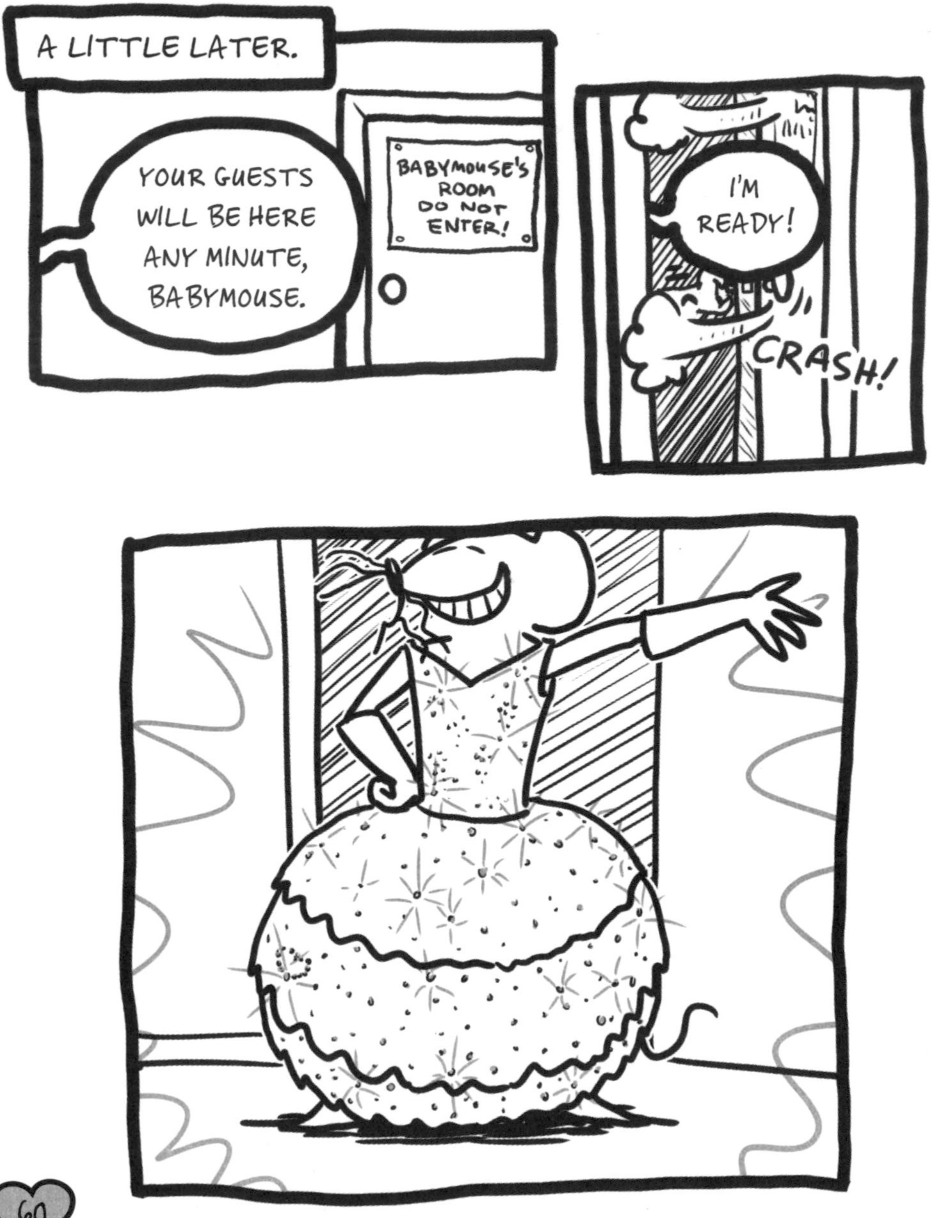
A LITTLE LATER.
YOUR GUESTS WILL BE HERE ANY MINUTE, BABYMOUSE.
BABYMOUSE'S ROOM DO NOT ENTER!
I'M READY!
CRASH!

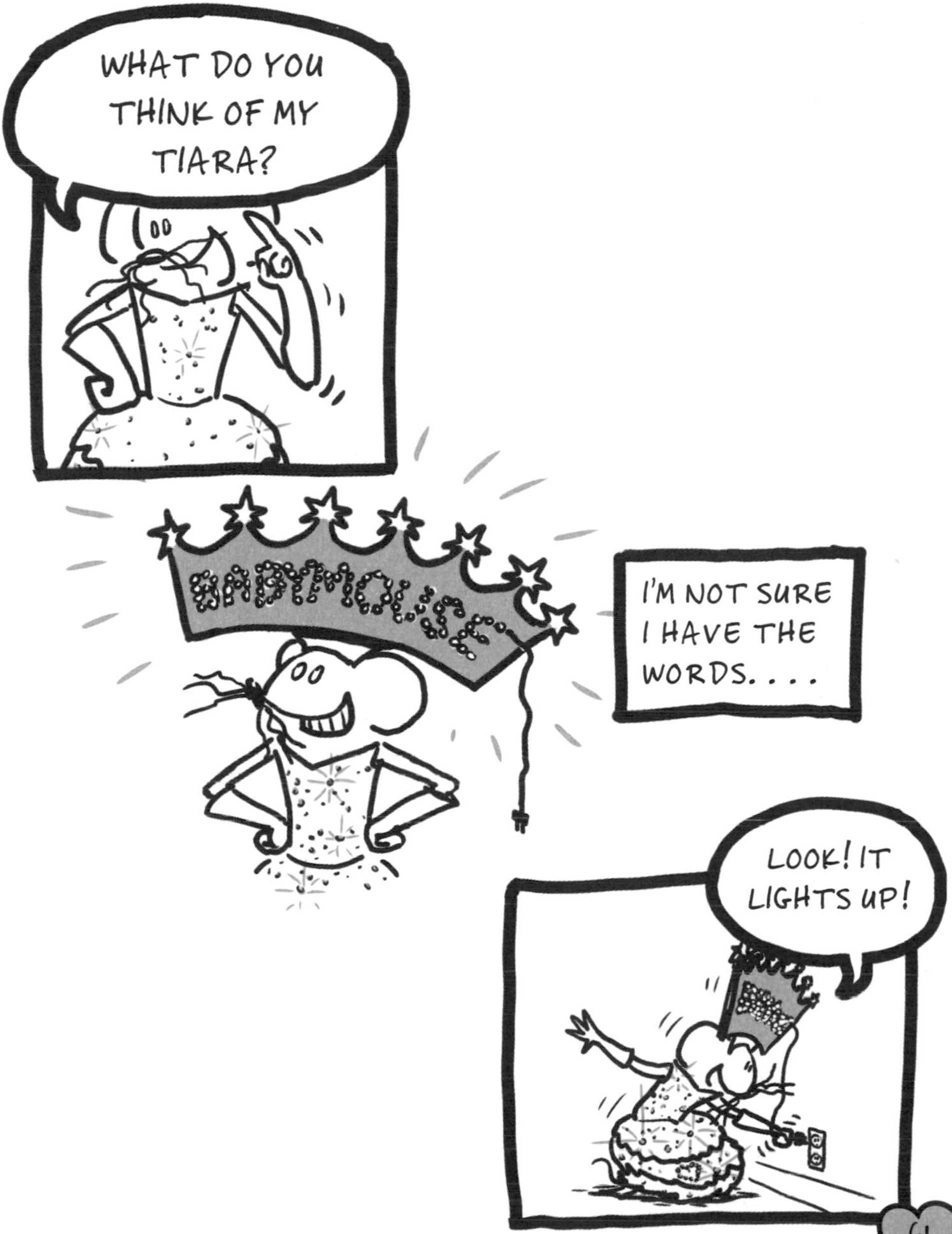
WHAT DO YOU THINK OF MY TIARA?
BABYMOUSE
I'M NOT SURE I HAVE THE WORDS. . . .
LOOK! IT LIGHTS UP!

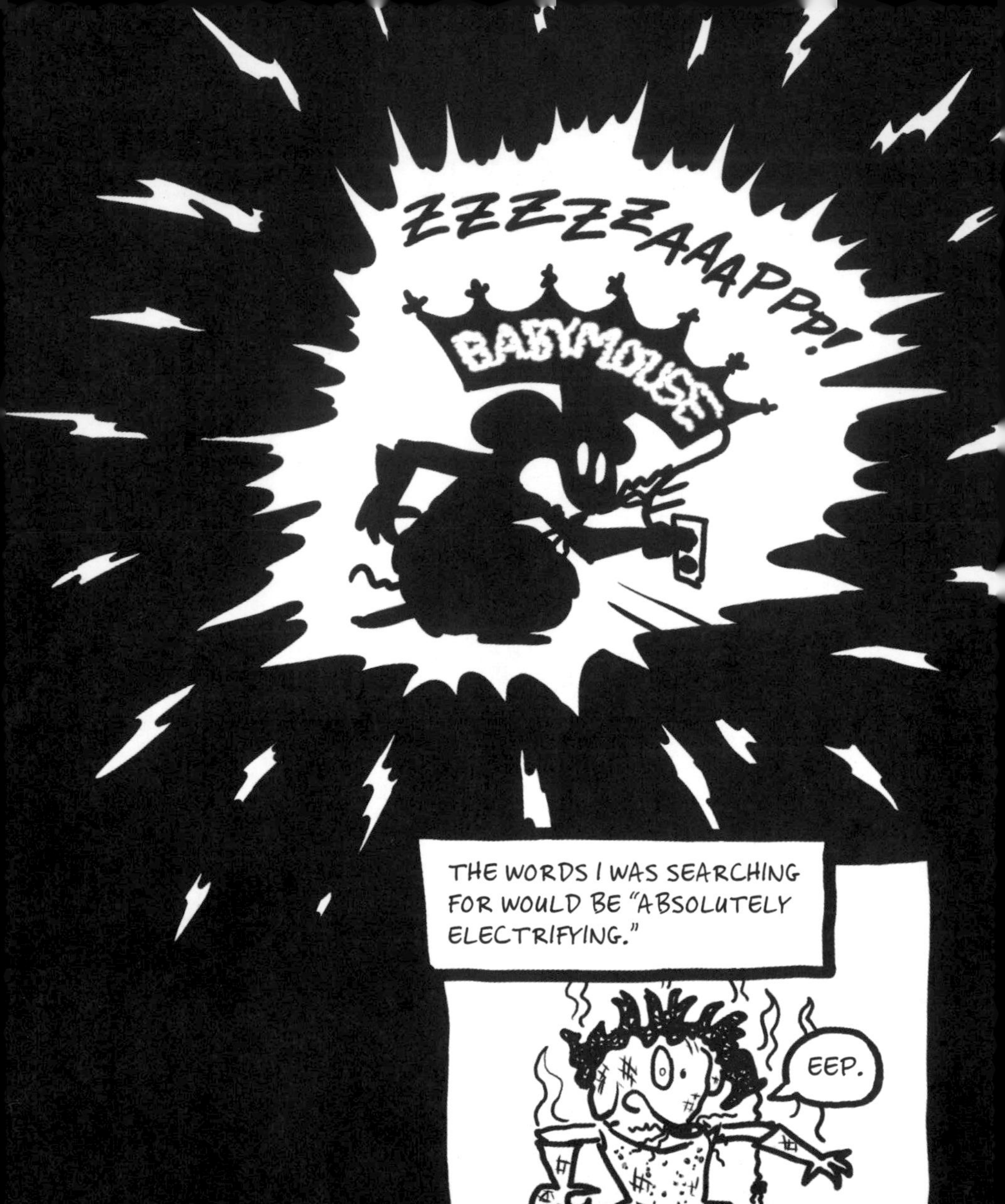
ZZZZZZAAAAPPP!
BABYMOUSE!
THE WORDS I WAS SEARCHING FOR WOULD BE "ABSOLUTELY ELECTRIFYING."
EEP.

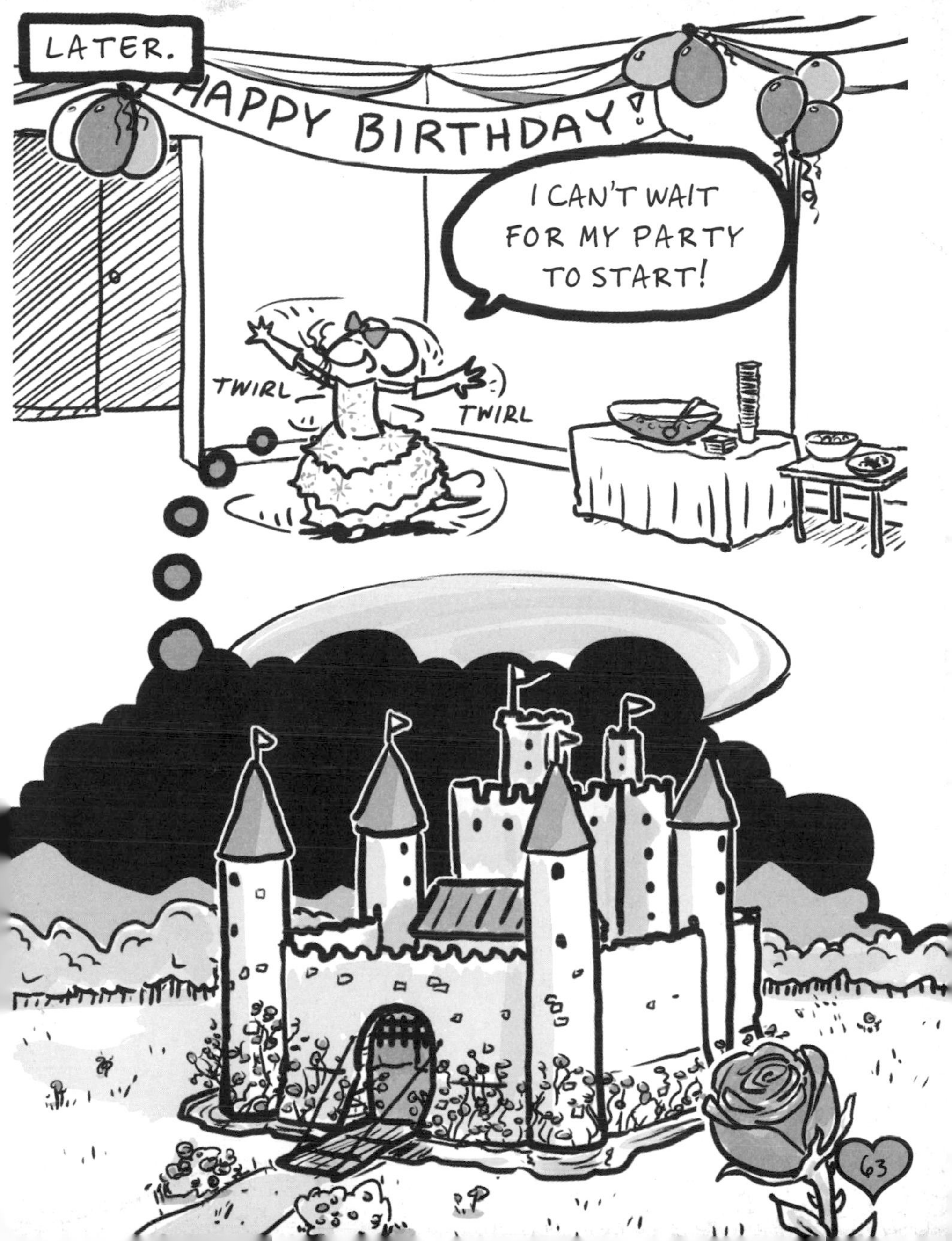

LATER.
HAPPY BIRTHDAY!
I CAN'T WAIT FOR MY PARTY TO START!
TWIRL
TWIRL

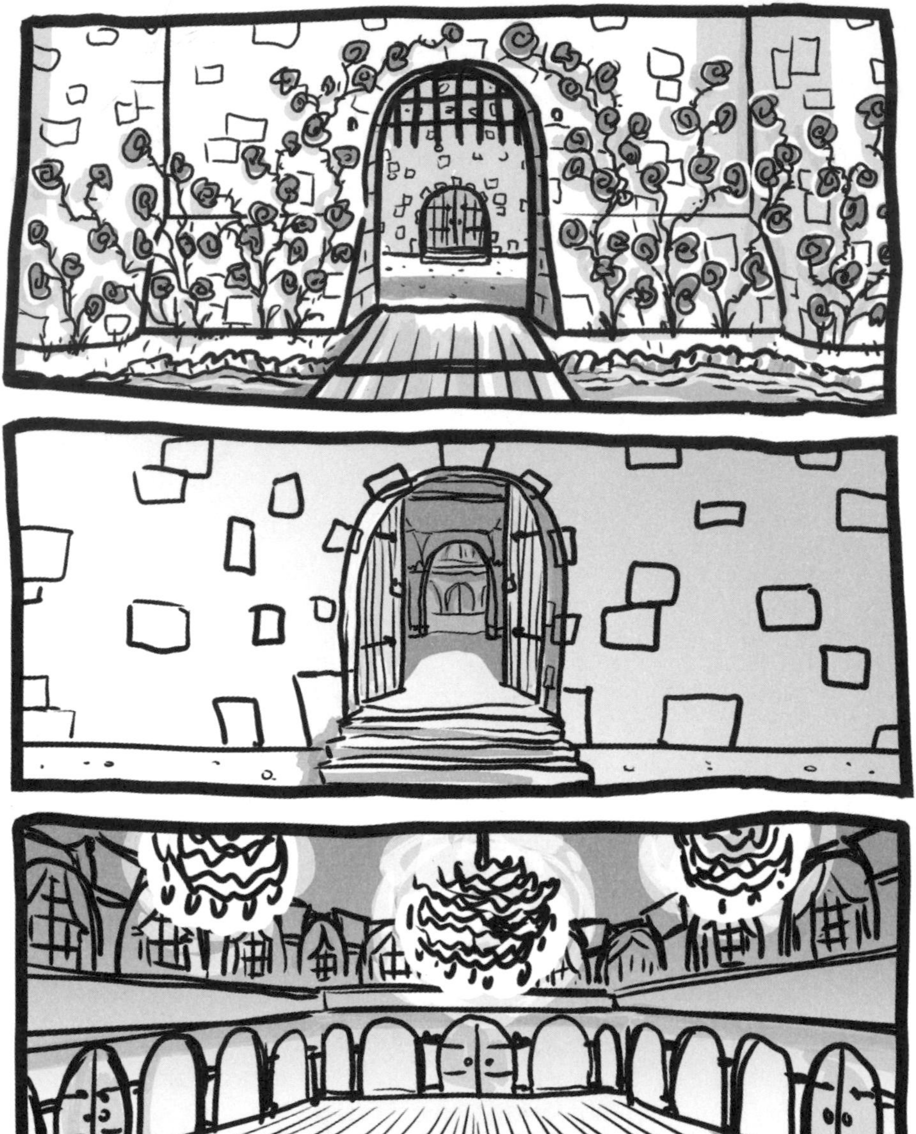

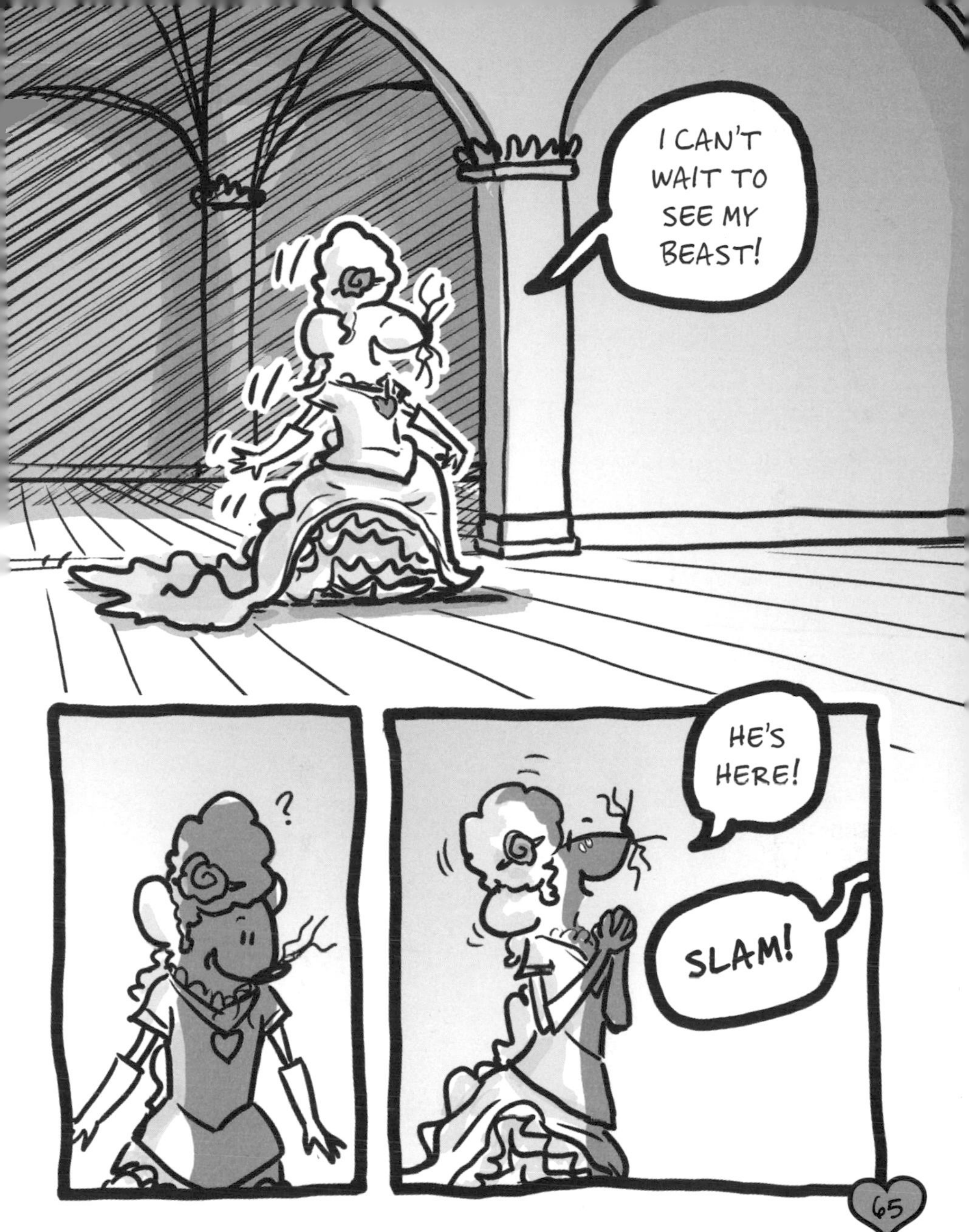
I CAN'T WAIT TO SEE MY BEAST!
?
HE'S HERE!
SLAM!

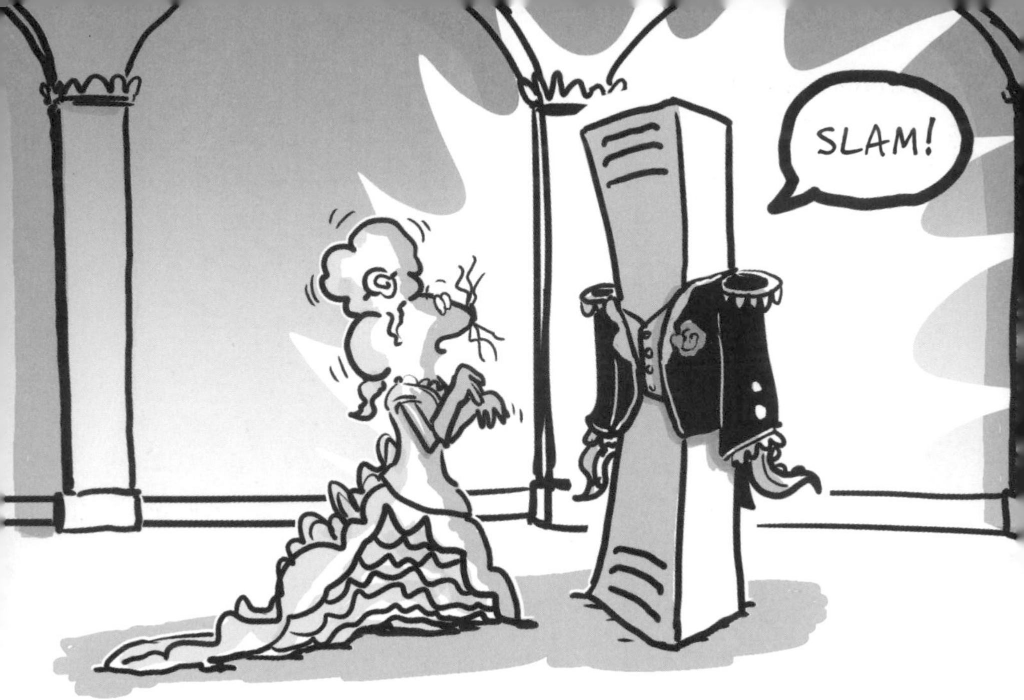
SLAM!

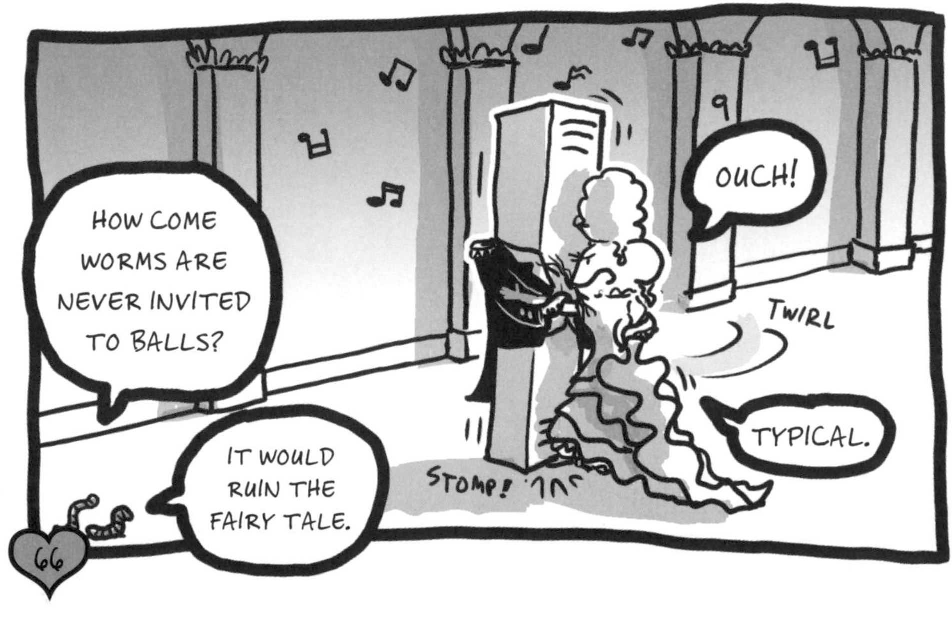
HOW COME WORMS ARE NEVER INVITED TO BALLS?
OUCH!
TWIRL
TYPICAL.
STOMP!
IT WOULD RUIN THE FAIRY TALE.

PARTY TIME.
TICK
TOCK
TICK
TOCK
TICK
TOCK
TICK
TOCK

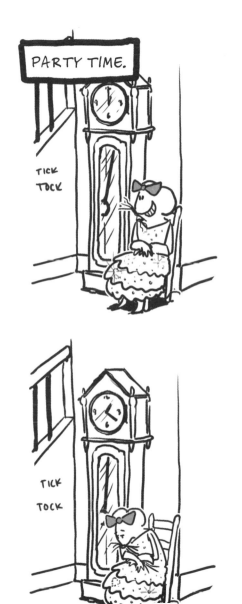

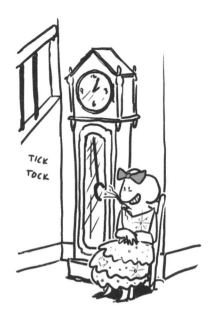

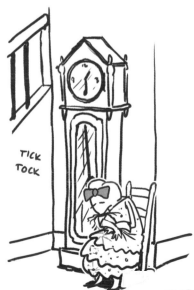

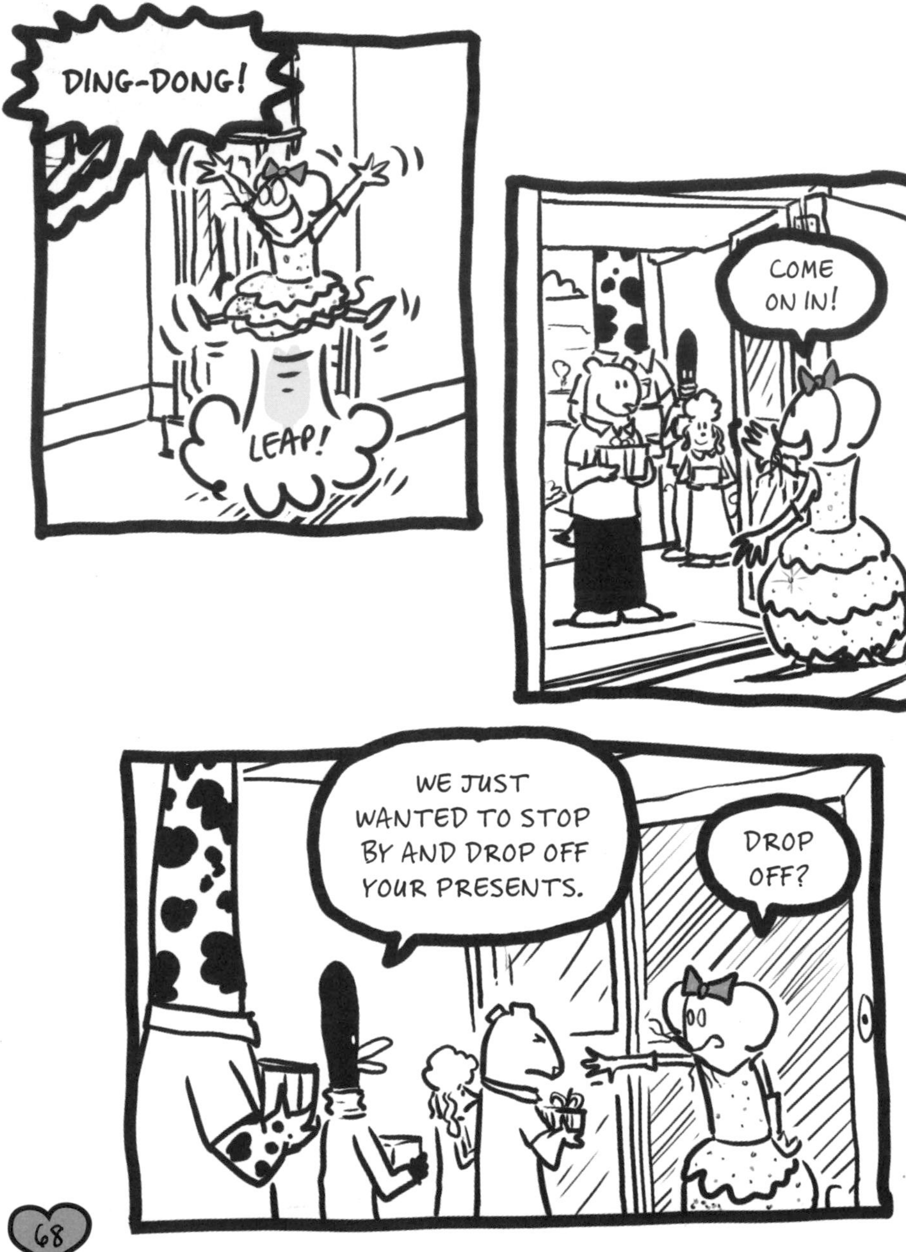
DING-DONG!
LEAP!
COME ON IN!
WE JUST WANTED TO STOP BY AND DROP OFF YOUR PRESENTS.
DROP OFF?

FELICIA SENT OUT HER INVITES FIRST, AND WE ALL RSVP'D BEFORE WE GOT YOURS.

MY MOM SAYS WE HAVE TO GO TO FELICIA'S PARTY BECAUSE IT'S GOOD MANNERS.

I TRIED TO TELL YOU BEFORE, BABYMOUSE, BUT I DIDN'T KNOW HOW.

SHRUG

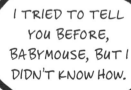

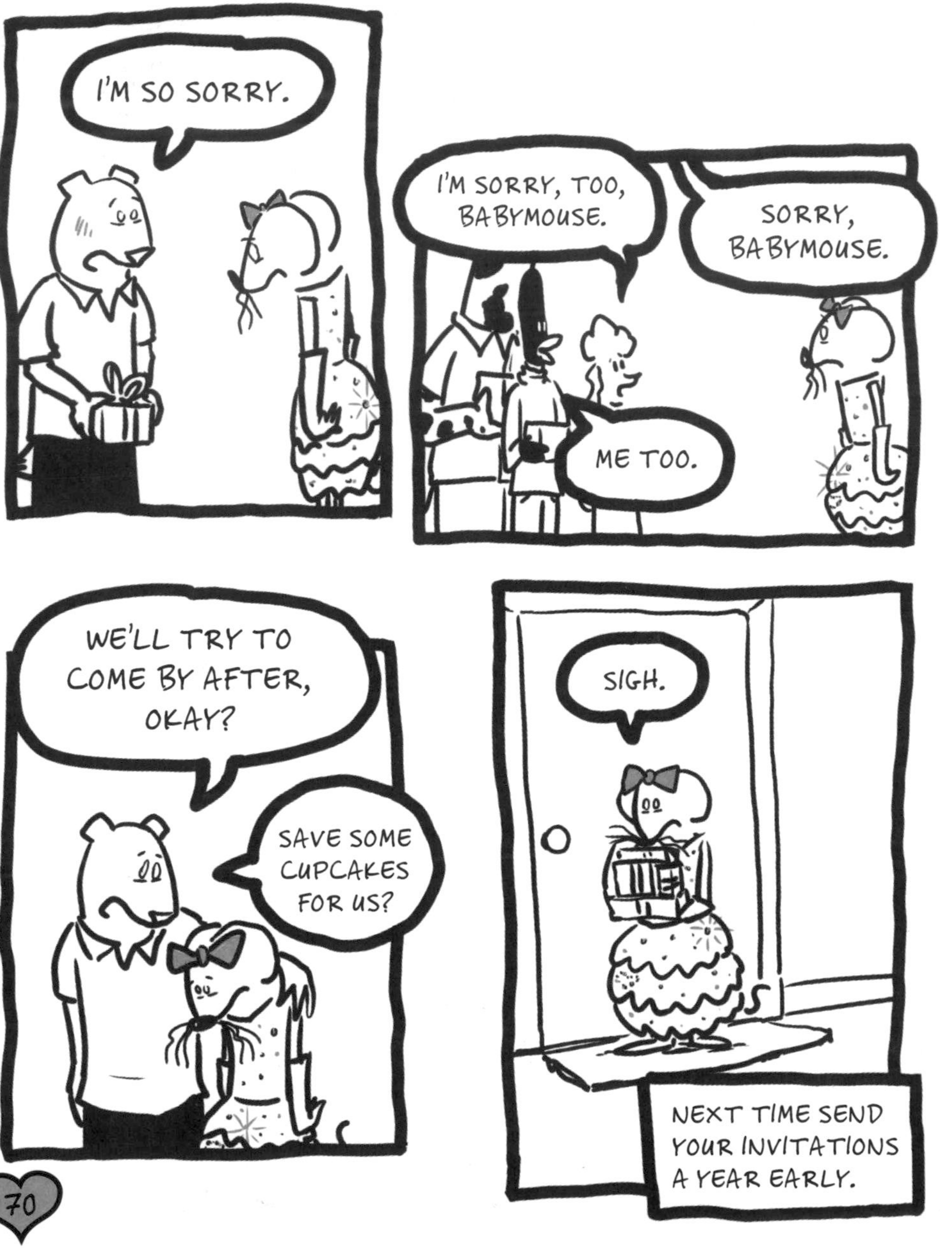
I'M SO SORRY.
I'M SORRY, TOO, BABYMOUSE.
SORRY, BABYMOUSE.
ME TOO.
WE'LL TRY TO COME BY AFTER, OKAY?
SAVE SOME CUPCAKES FOR US?
SIGH.
NEXT TIME SEND YOUR INVITATIONS A YEAR EARLY.

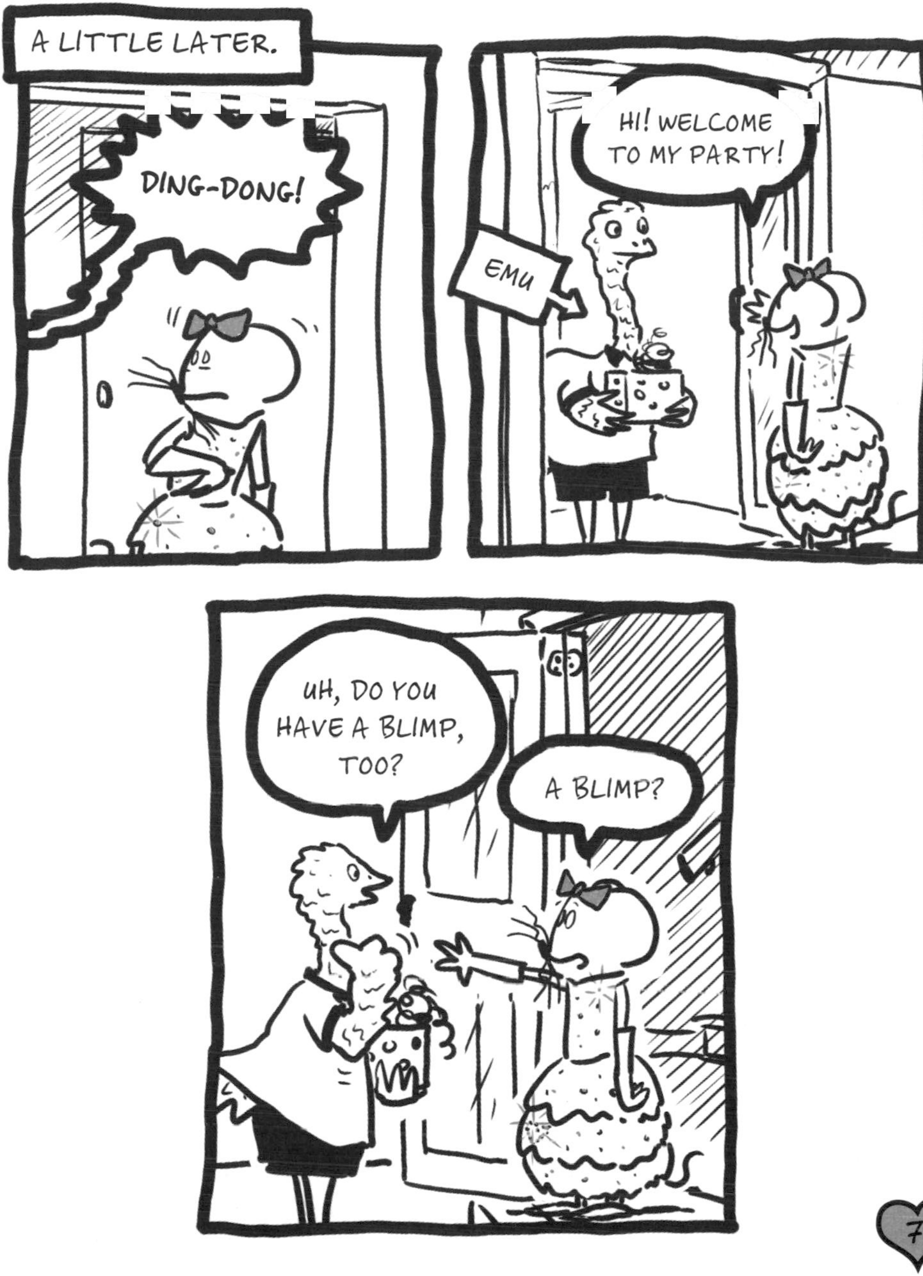
A LITTLE LATER.
DING-DONG!
HI! WELCOME TO MY PARTY!
EMU
UH, DO YOU HAVE A BLIMP, TOO?
A BLIMP?

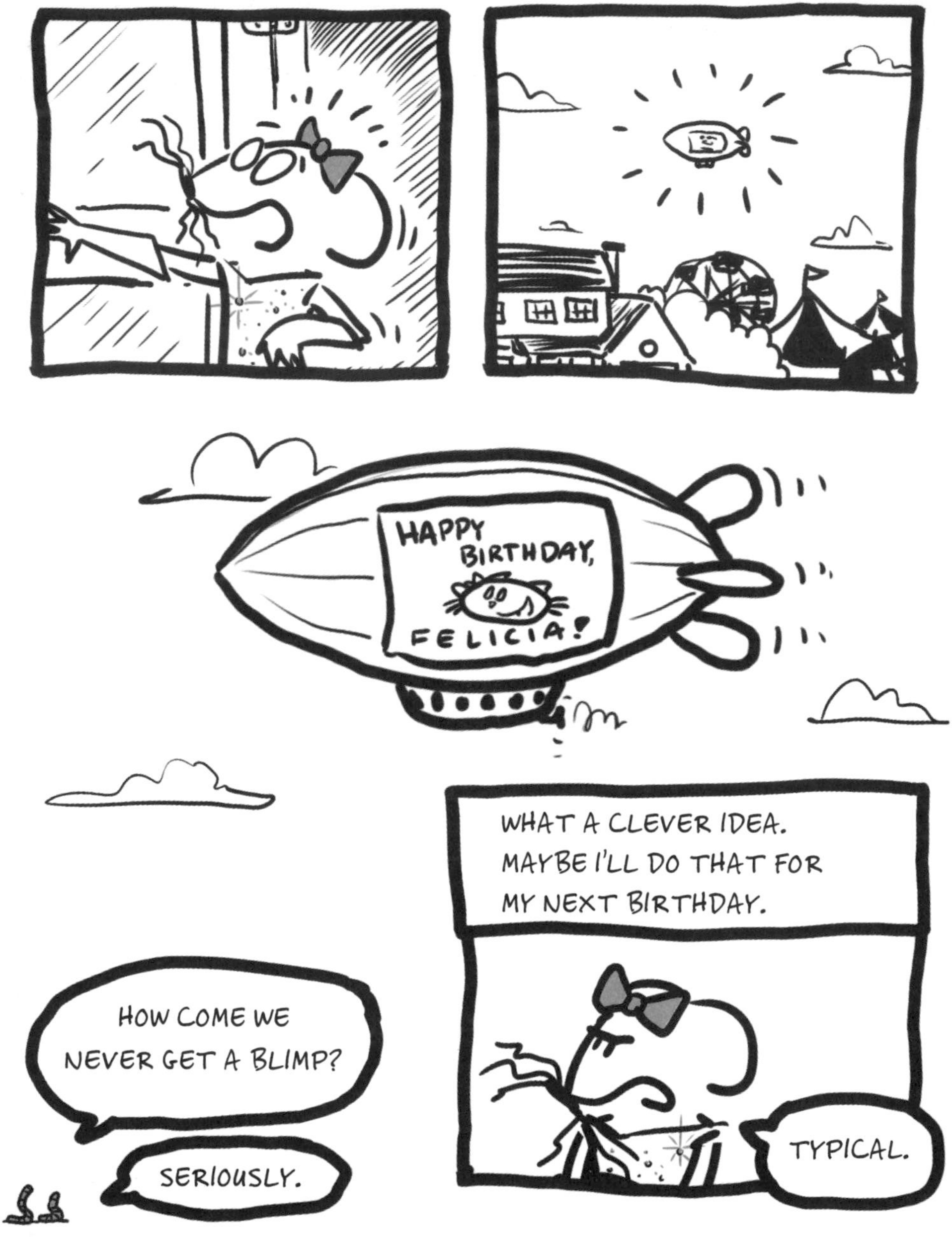
HAPPY BIRTHDAY, FELICIA!
WHAT A CLEVER IDEA. MAYBE I'LL DO THAT FOR MY NEXT BIRTHDAY.
HOW COME WE NEVER GET A BLIMP?
SERIOUSLY.
TYPICAL.

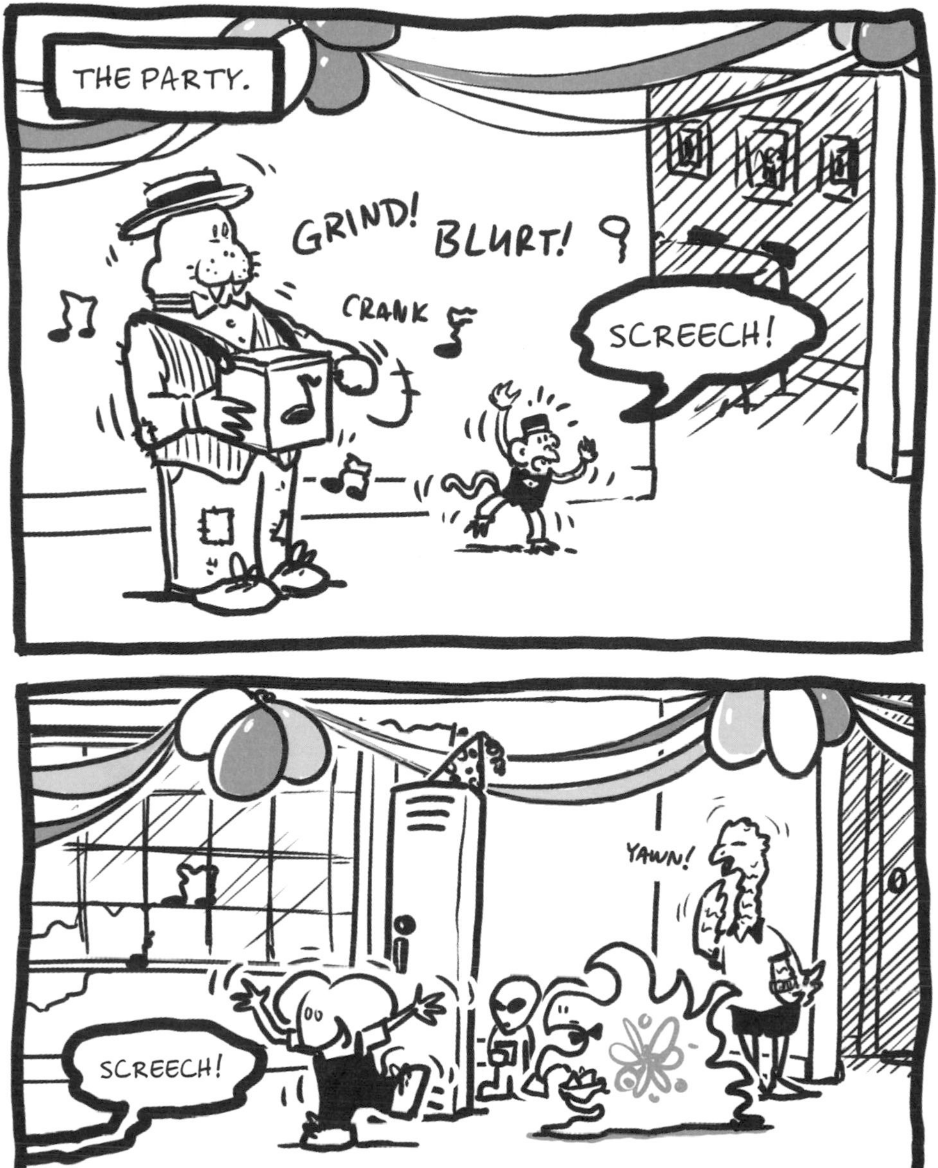
THE PARTY.
GRIND!
BLURT!
CRANK
SCREECH!
YAWN!
SCREECH!

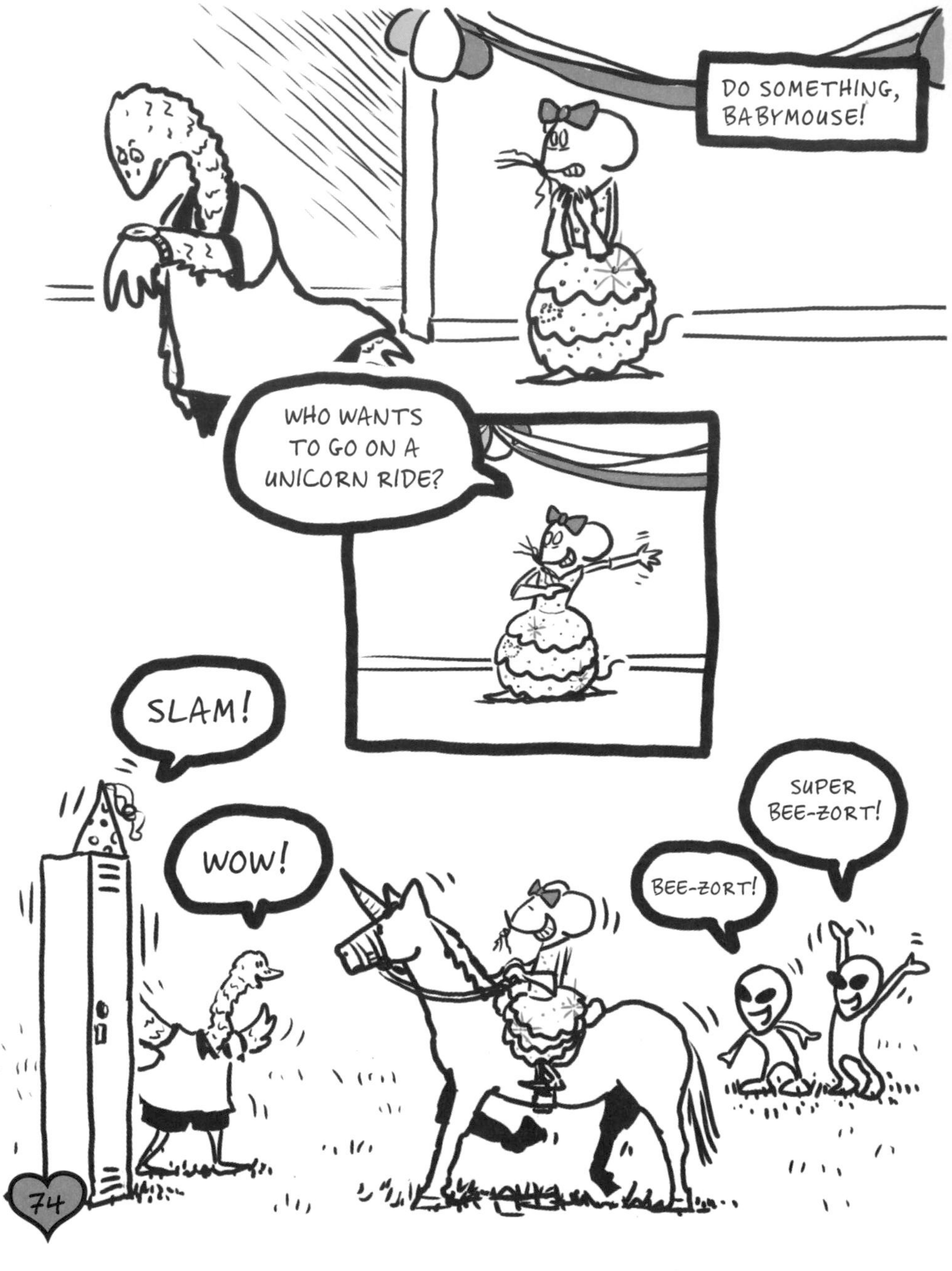

DO SOMETHING, BABYMOUSE!
WHO WANTS TO GO ON A UNICORN RIDE?
SLAM!
WOW!
BEE-ZORT!
SUPER BEE-ZORT!

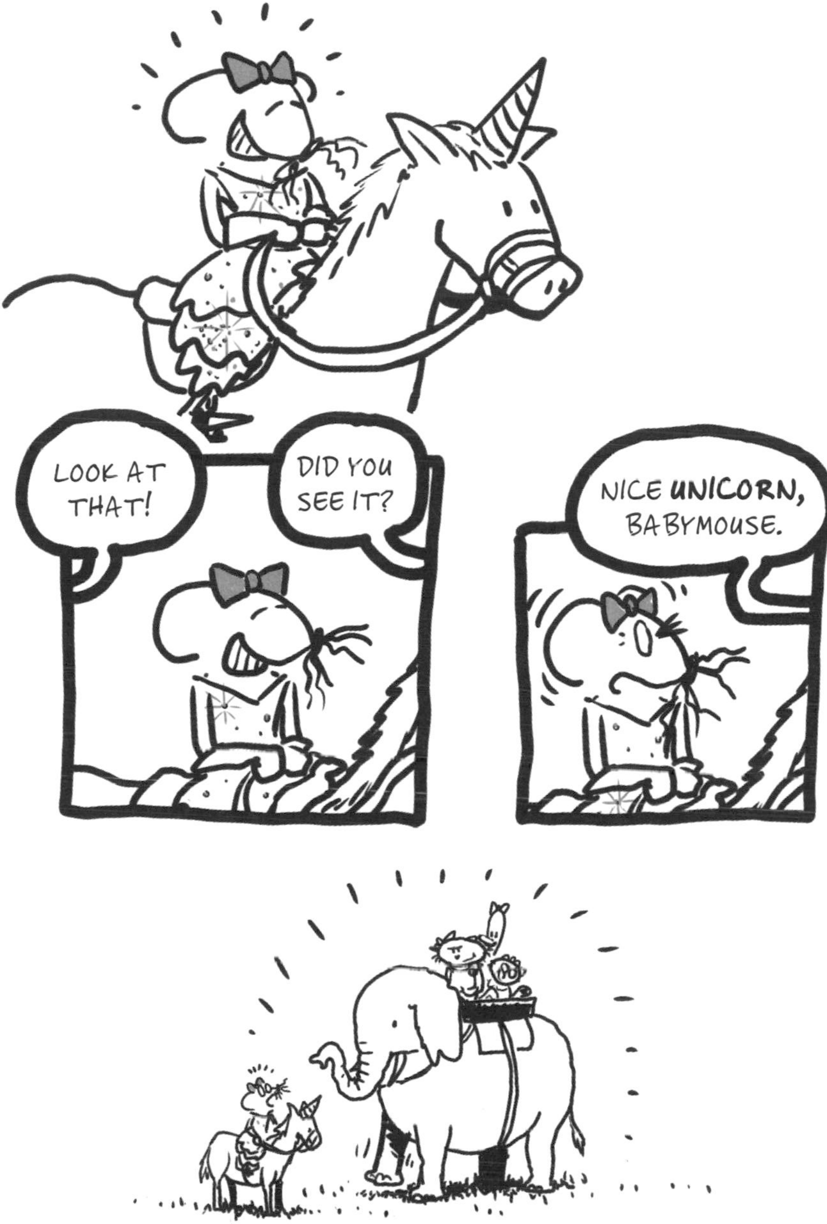
LOOK AT THAT!
DID YOU SEE IT?
NICE **UNICORN**, BABYMOUSE.

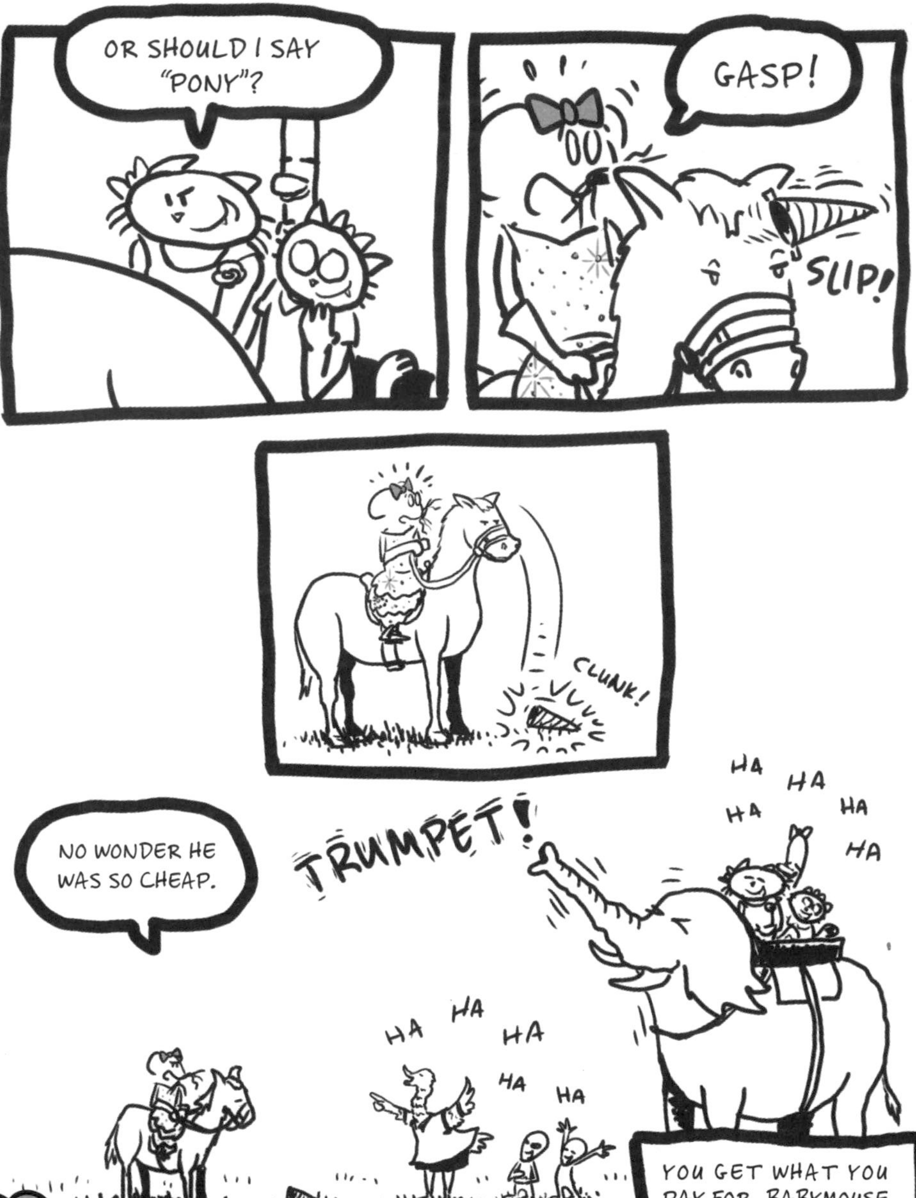

OR SHOULD I SAY "PONY"?
GASP!
SLIP!
CLUNK!
NO WONDER HE WAS SO CHEAP.
TRUMPET!
HA HA HA HA HA
HA HA HA HA HA
YOU GET WHAT YOU PAY FOR, BABYMOUSE.

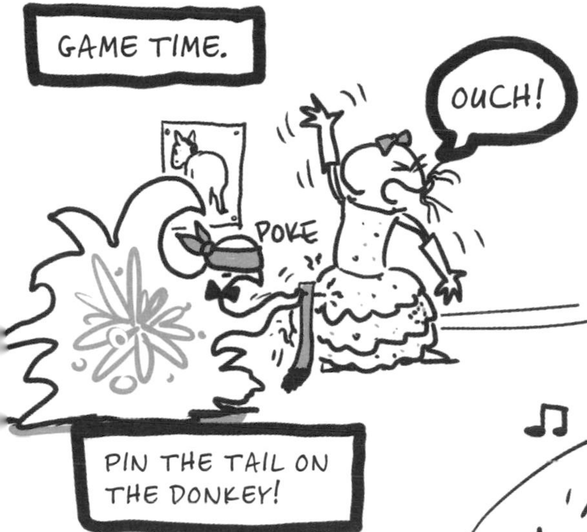
GAME TIME.
OUCH!
POKE
PIN THE TAIL ON THE DONKEY!

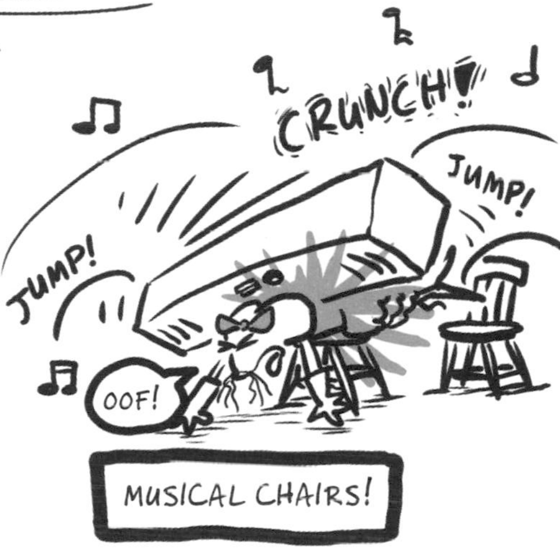
CRUNCH!
JUMP!
JUMP!
OOF!
MUSICAL CHAIRS!

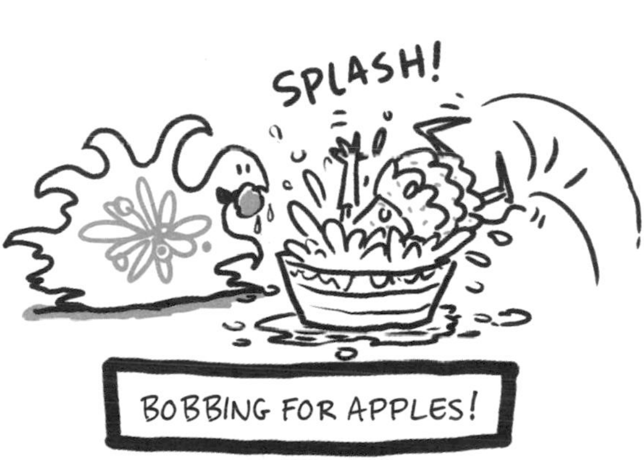
SPLASH!
BOBBING FOR APPLES!

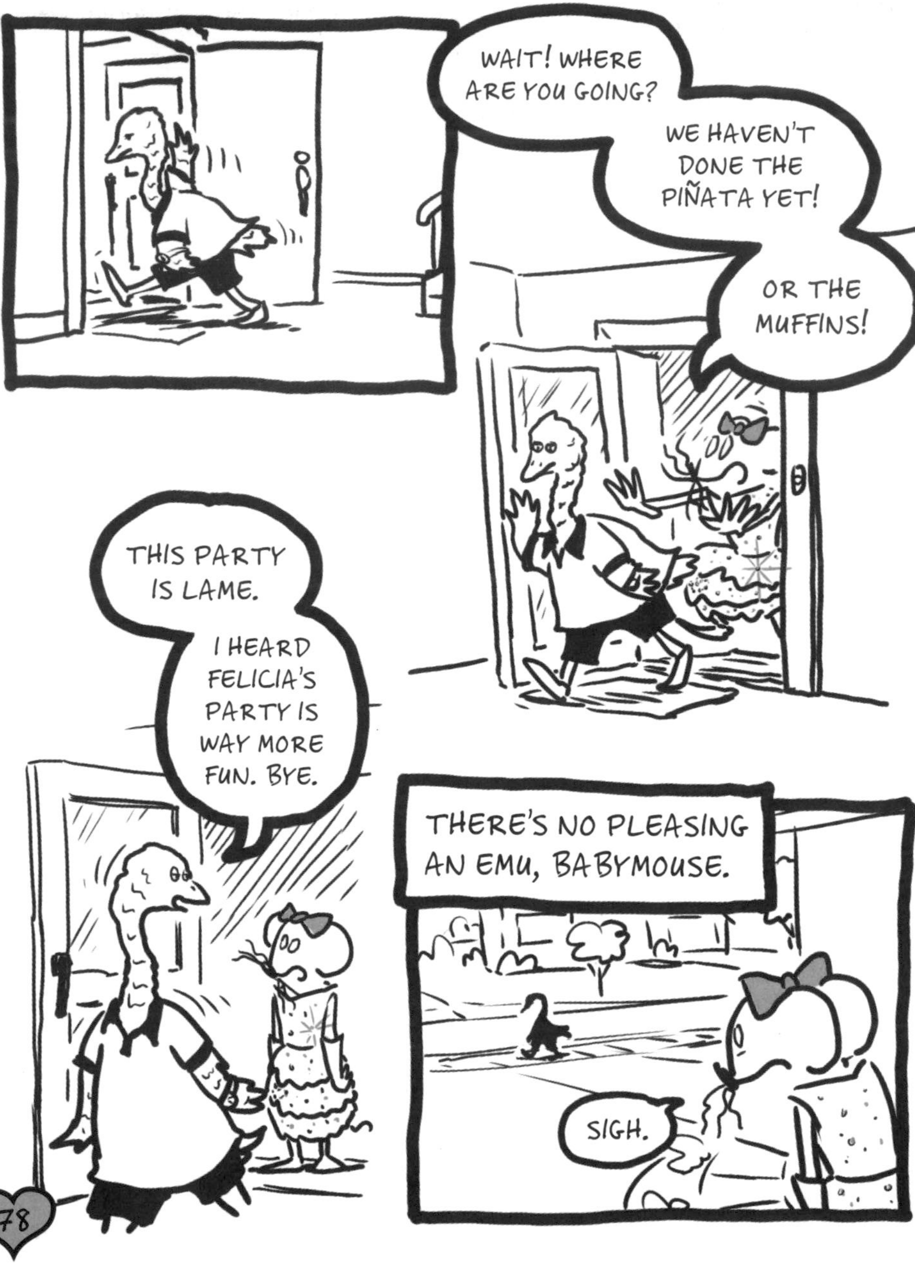

WAIT! WHERE ARE YOU GOING?
WE HAVEN'T DONE THE PIÑATA YET!
OR THE MUFFINS!
THIS PARTY IS LAME.
I HEARD FELICIA'S PARTY IS WAY MORE FUN. BYE.
THERE'S NO PLEASING AN EMU, BABYMOUSE.
SIGH.

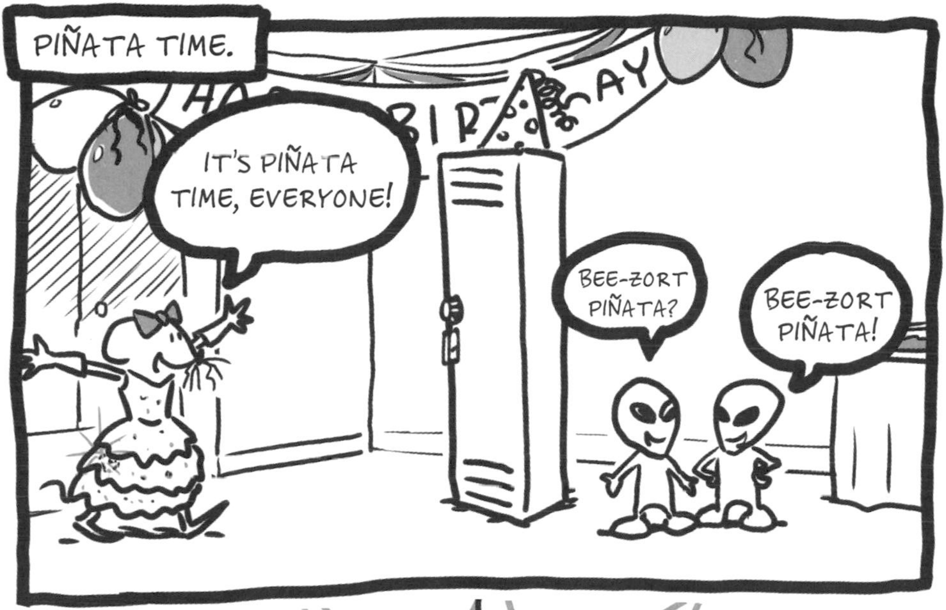
PIÑATA TIME.
IT'S PIÑATA TIME, EVERYONE!
BEE-ZORT PIÑATA?
BEE-ZORT PIÑATA!

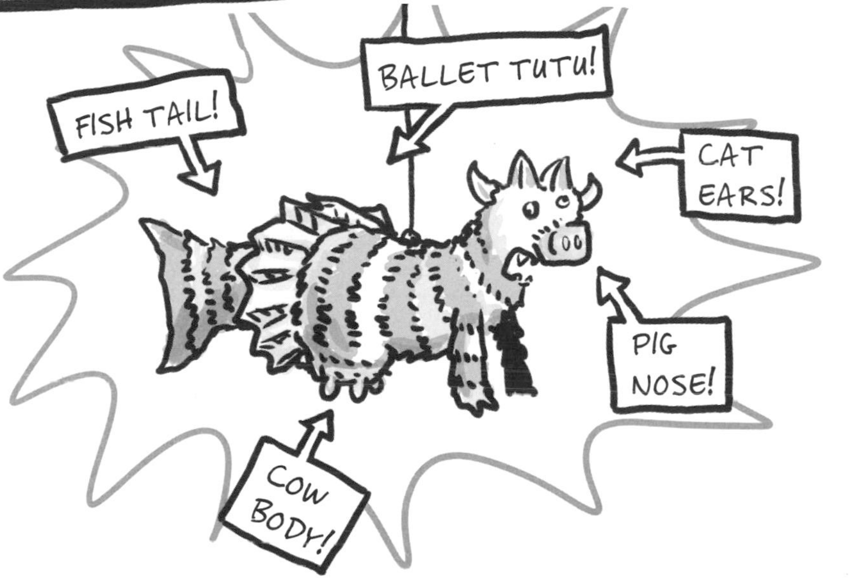
BALLET TUTU!
FISH TAIL!
CAT EARS!
PIG NOSE!
COW BODY!

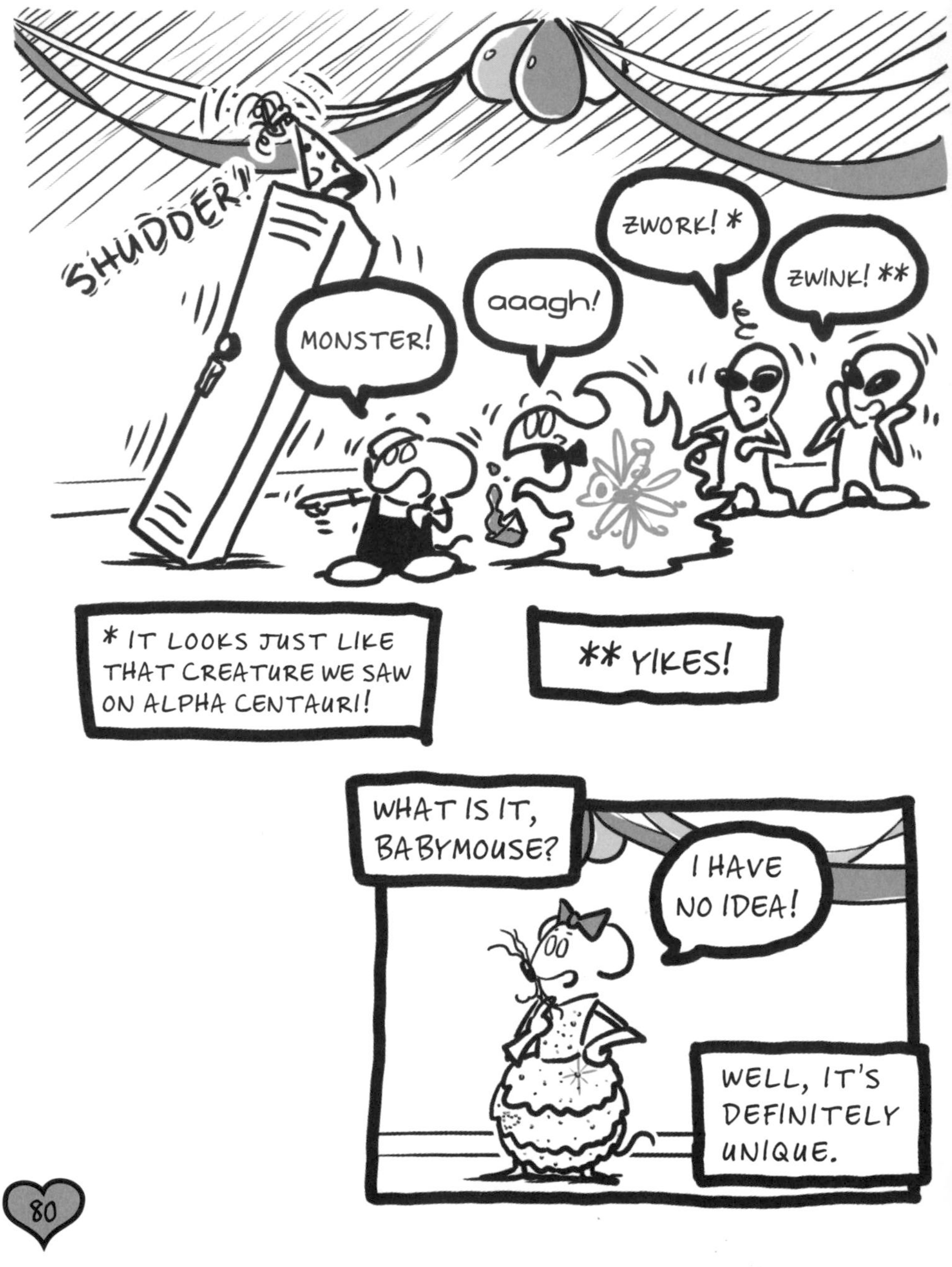

SHUDDER!!
MONSTER!
aaagh!
ZWORK! *
ZWINK! **
* IT LOOKS JUST LIKE THAT CREATURE WE SAW ON ALPHA CENTAURI!
** YIKES!
WHAT IS IT, BABYMOUSE?
I HAVE NO IDEA!
WELL, IT'S DEFINITELY UNIQUE.

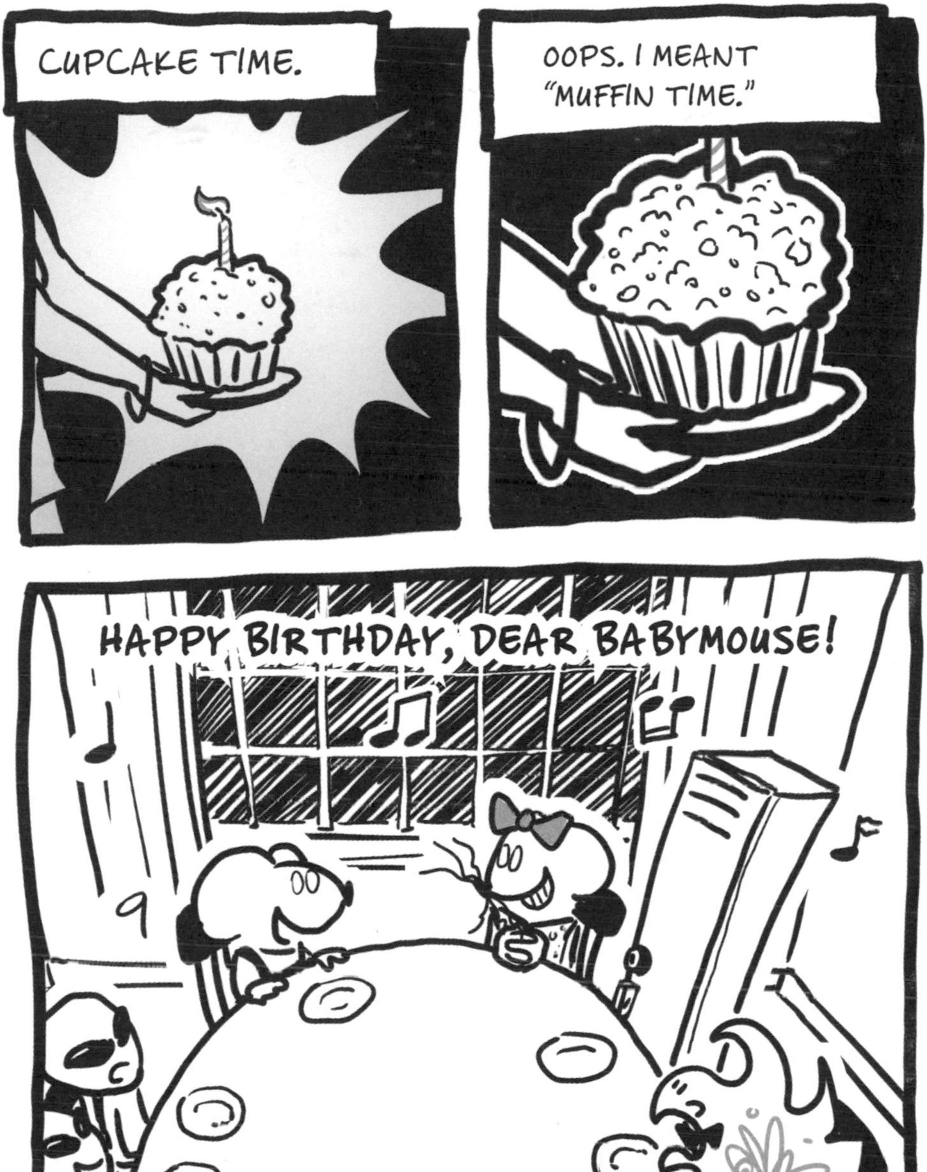
CUPCAKE TIME.
OOPS. I MEANT "MUFFIN TIME."
HAPPY BIRTHDAY, DEAR BABYMOUSE!

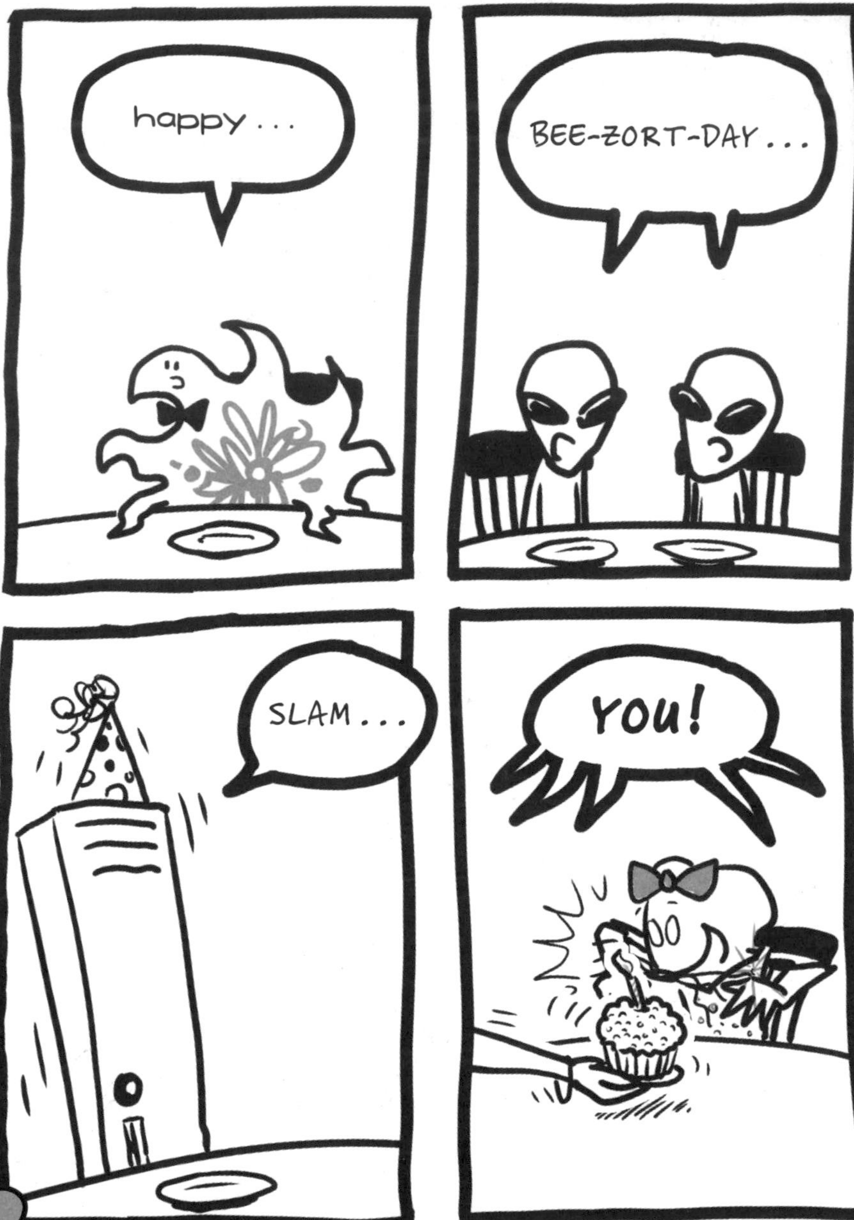
happy . . .
BEE-ZORT-DAY . . .
SLAM . . .
YOU!

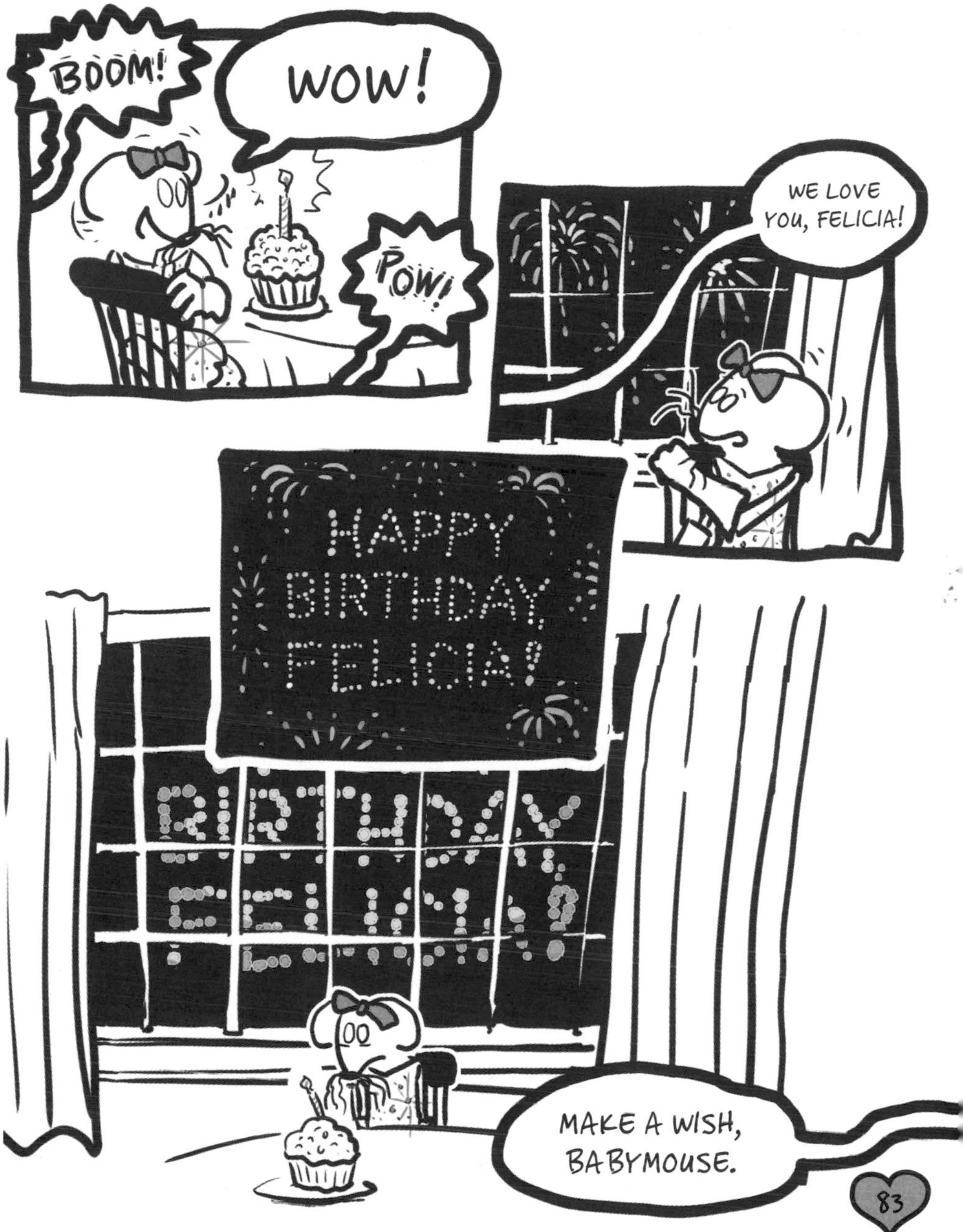
BOOM!
WOW!
POW!
WE LOVE YOU, FELICIA!
HAPPY BIRTHDAY, FELICIA!
MAKE A WISH, BABYMOUSE.

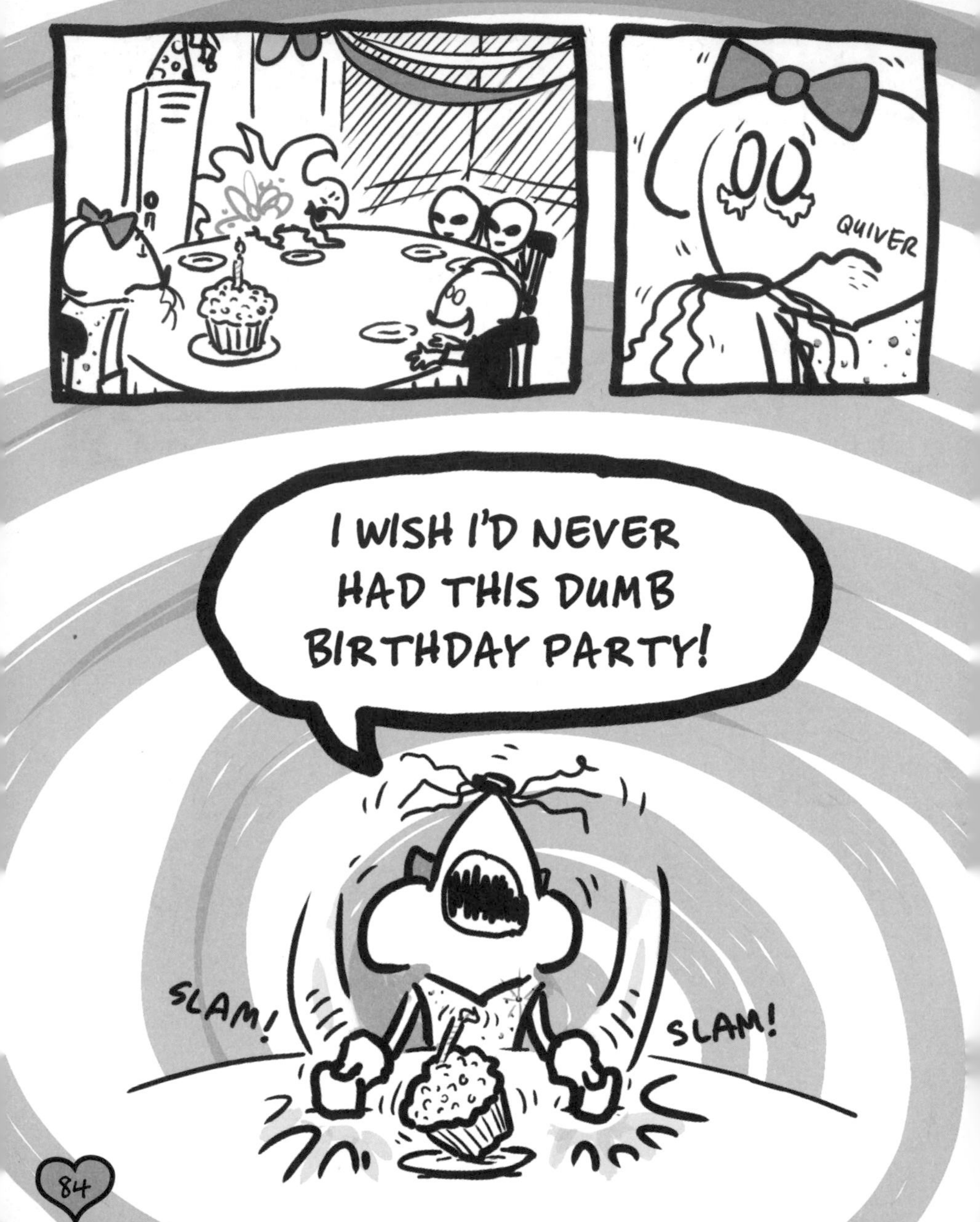
QUIVER
I WISH I'D NEVER HAD THIS DUMB BIRTHDAY PARTY!
SLAM!
SLAM!

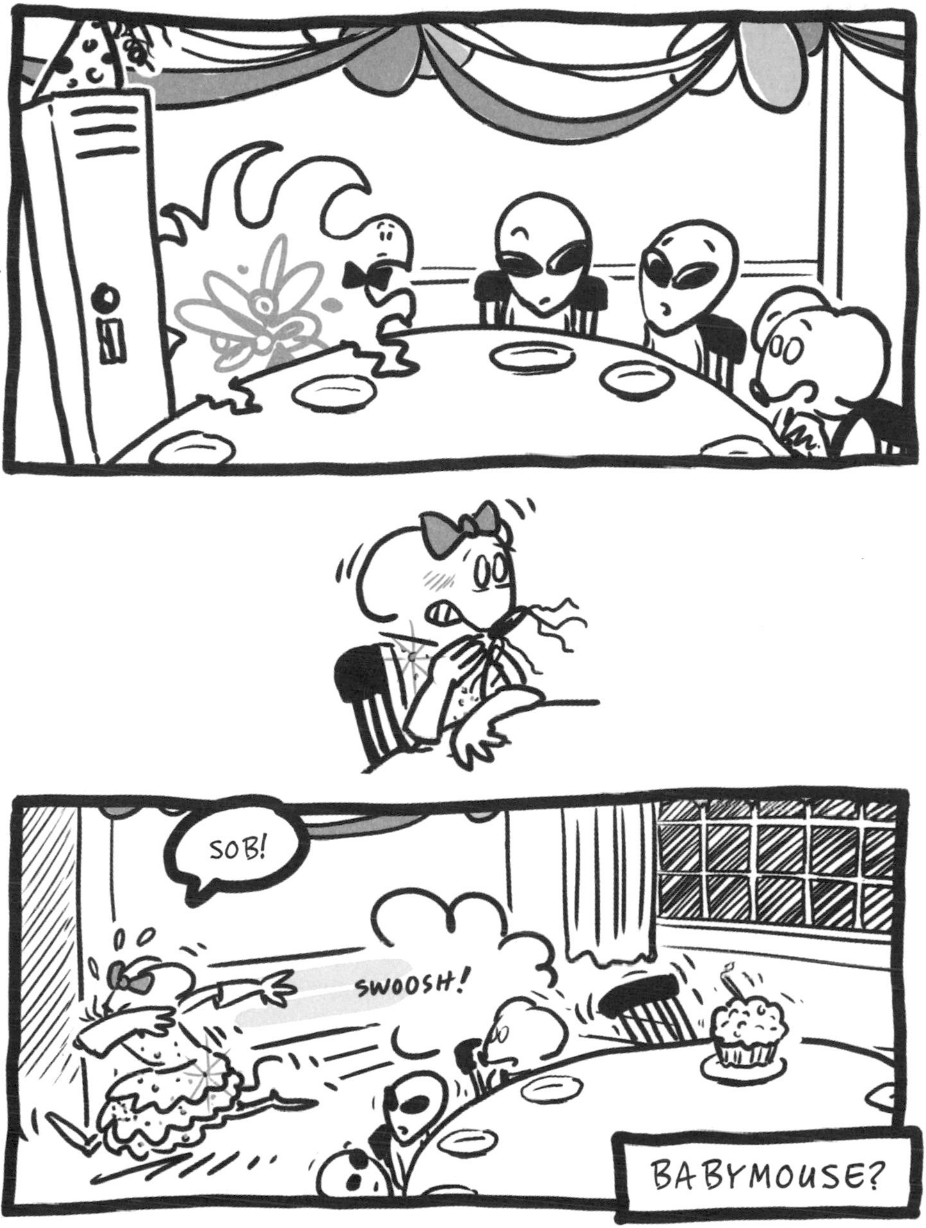
SOB!
SWOOSH!
BABYMOUSE?

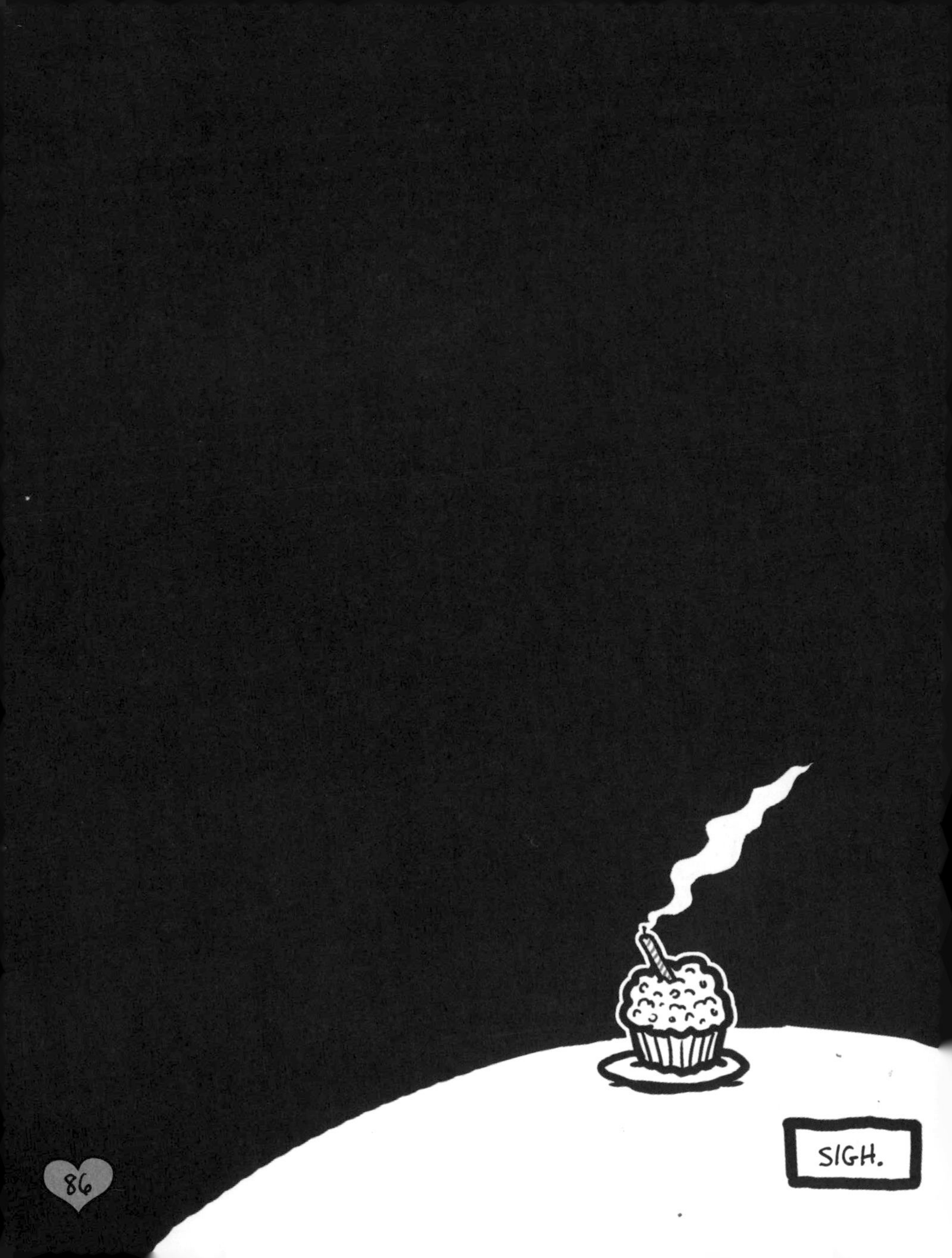
SIGH.

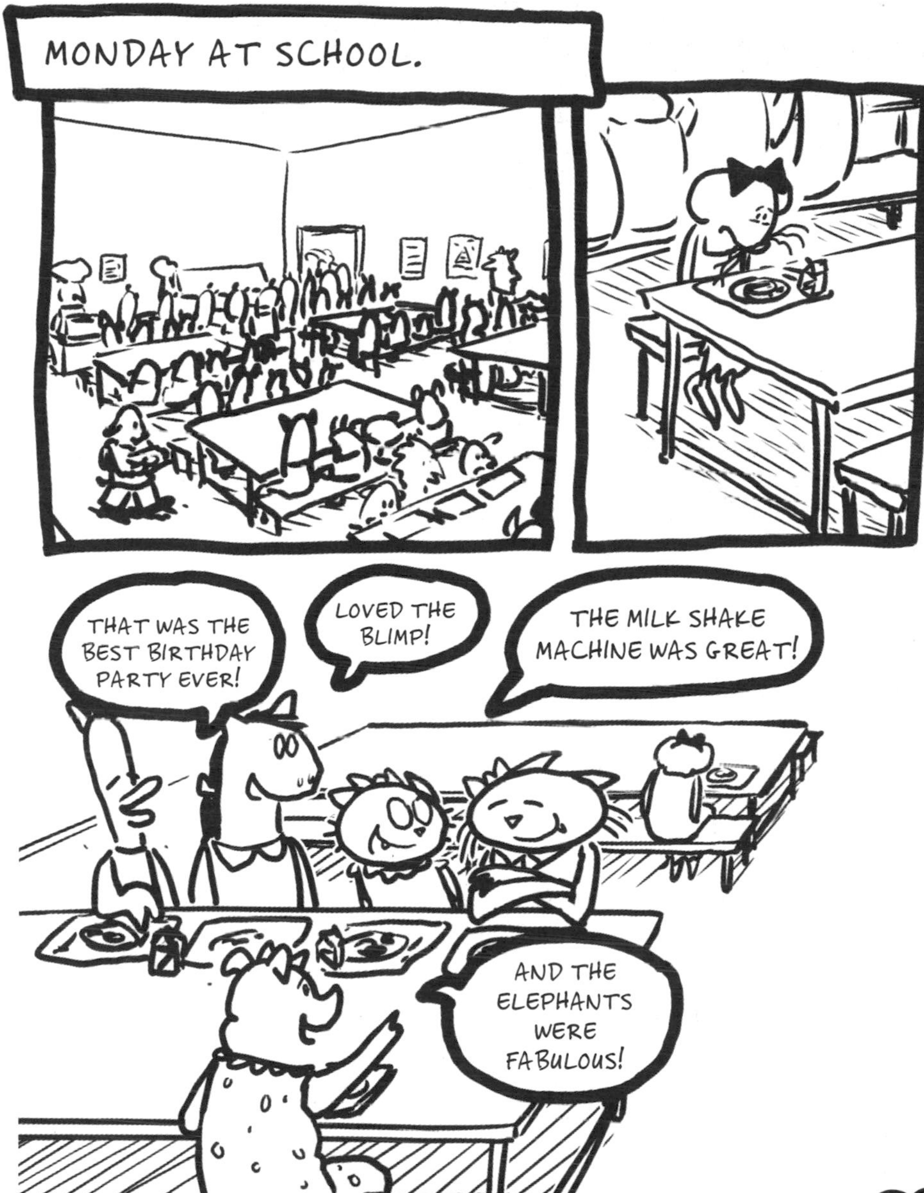
MONDAY AT SCHOOL.
THAT WAS THE BEST BIRTHDAY PARTY EVER!
LOVED THE BLIMP!
THE MILK SHAKE MACHINE WAS GREAT!
AND THE ELEPHANTS WERE FABULOUS!

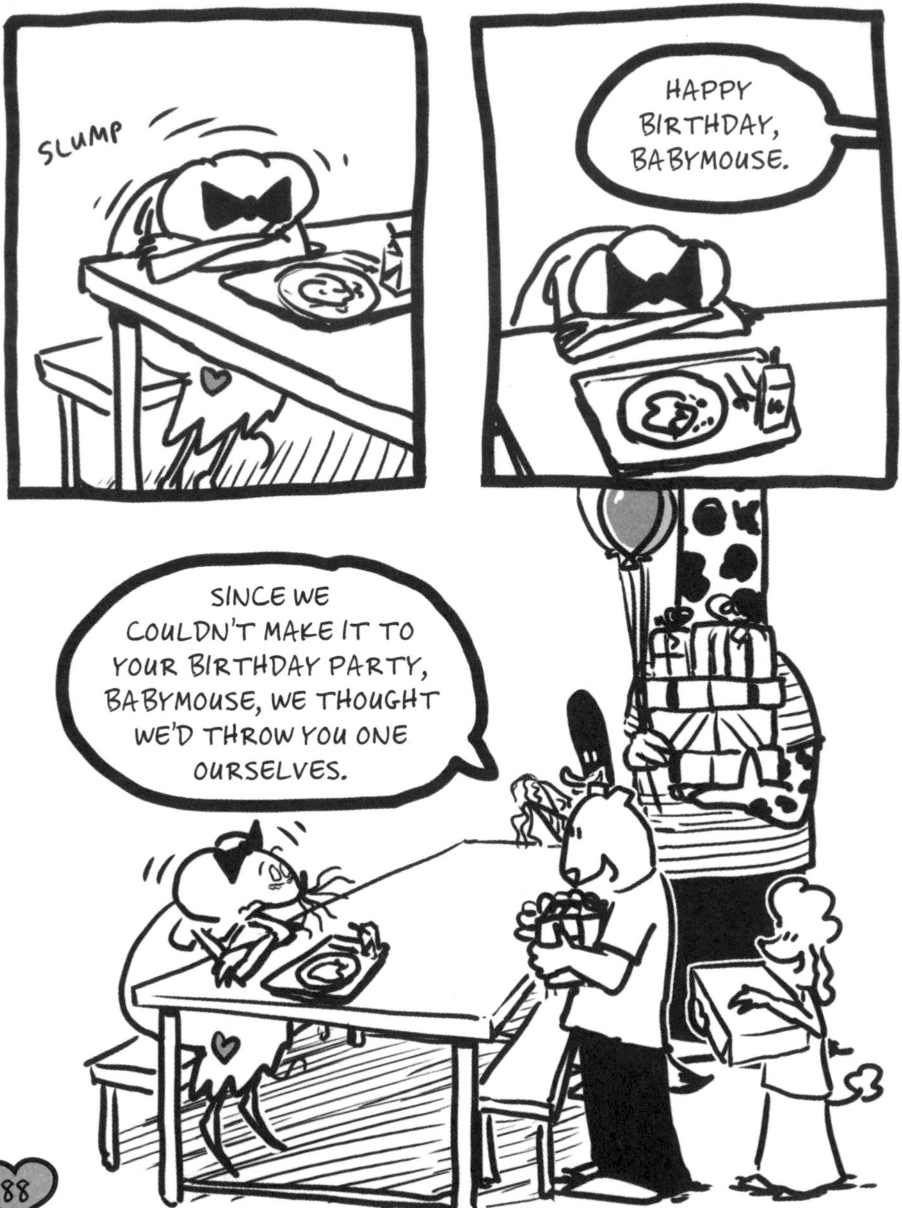
SLUMP
HAPPY BIRTHDAY, BABYMOUSE.
SINCE WE COULDN'T MAKE IT TO YOUR BIRTHDAY PARTY, BABYMOUSE, WE THOUGHT WE'D THROW YOU ONE OURSELVES.

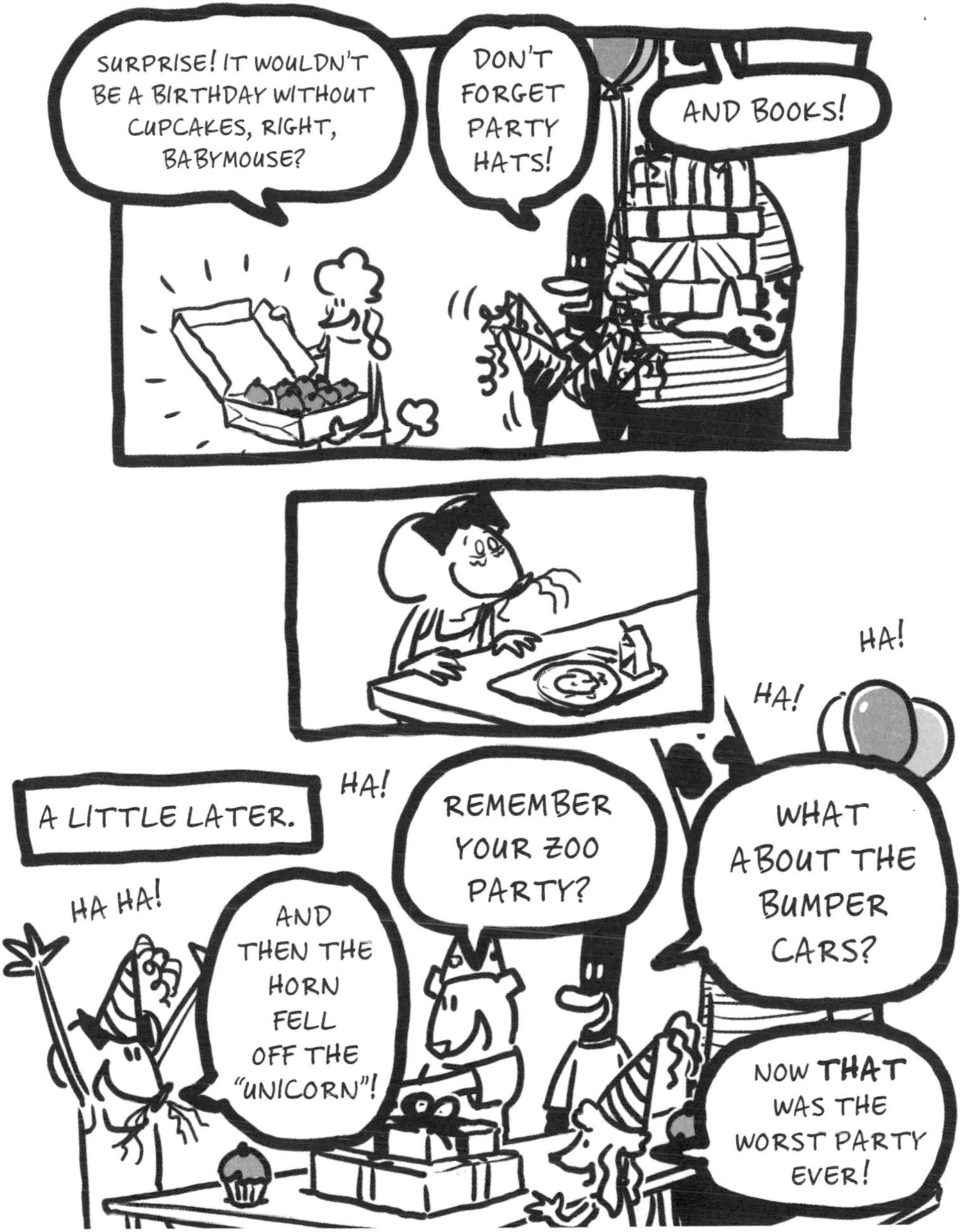
SURPRISE! IT WOULDN'T BE A BIRTHDAY WITHOUT CUPCAKES, RIGHT, BABYMOUSE?
DON'T FORGET PARTY HATS!
AND BOOKS!
A LITTLE LATER.
HA!
HA!
HA!
HA HA!
AND THEN THE HORN FELL OFF THE "UNICORN"!
REMEMBER YOUR ZOO PARTY?
WHAT ABOUT THE BUMPER CARS?
NOW **THAT** WAS THE WORST PARTY EVER!

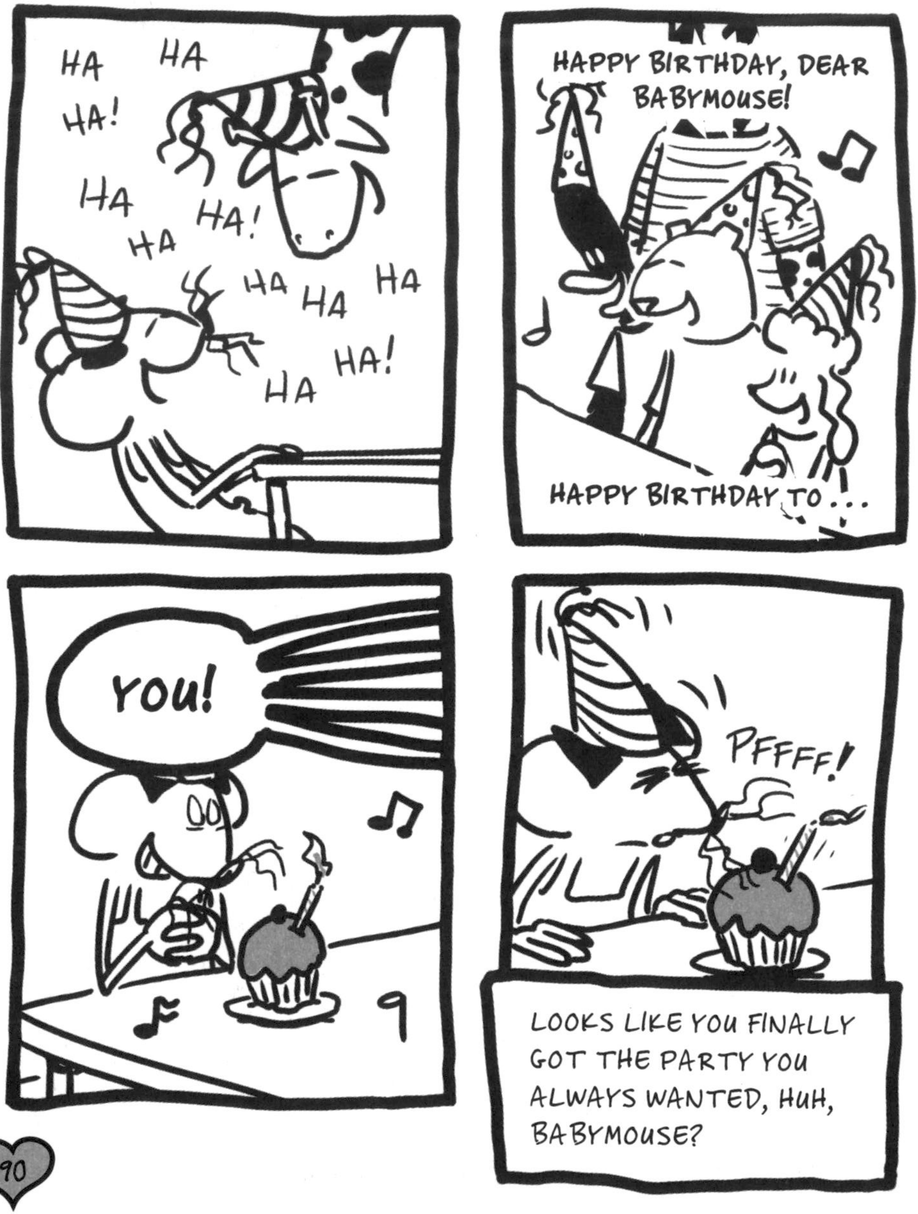
HA HA HA!
HA HA! HA
HA HA HA
HA! HA
HAPPY BIRTHDAY, DEAR BABYMOUSE!
HAPPY BIRTHDAY TO...
YOU!
PFFFFF!
LOOKS LIKE YOU FINALLY GOT THE PARTY YOU ALWAYS WANTED, HUH, BABYMOUSE?

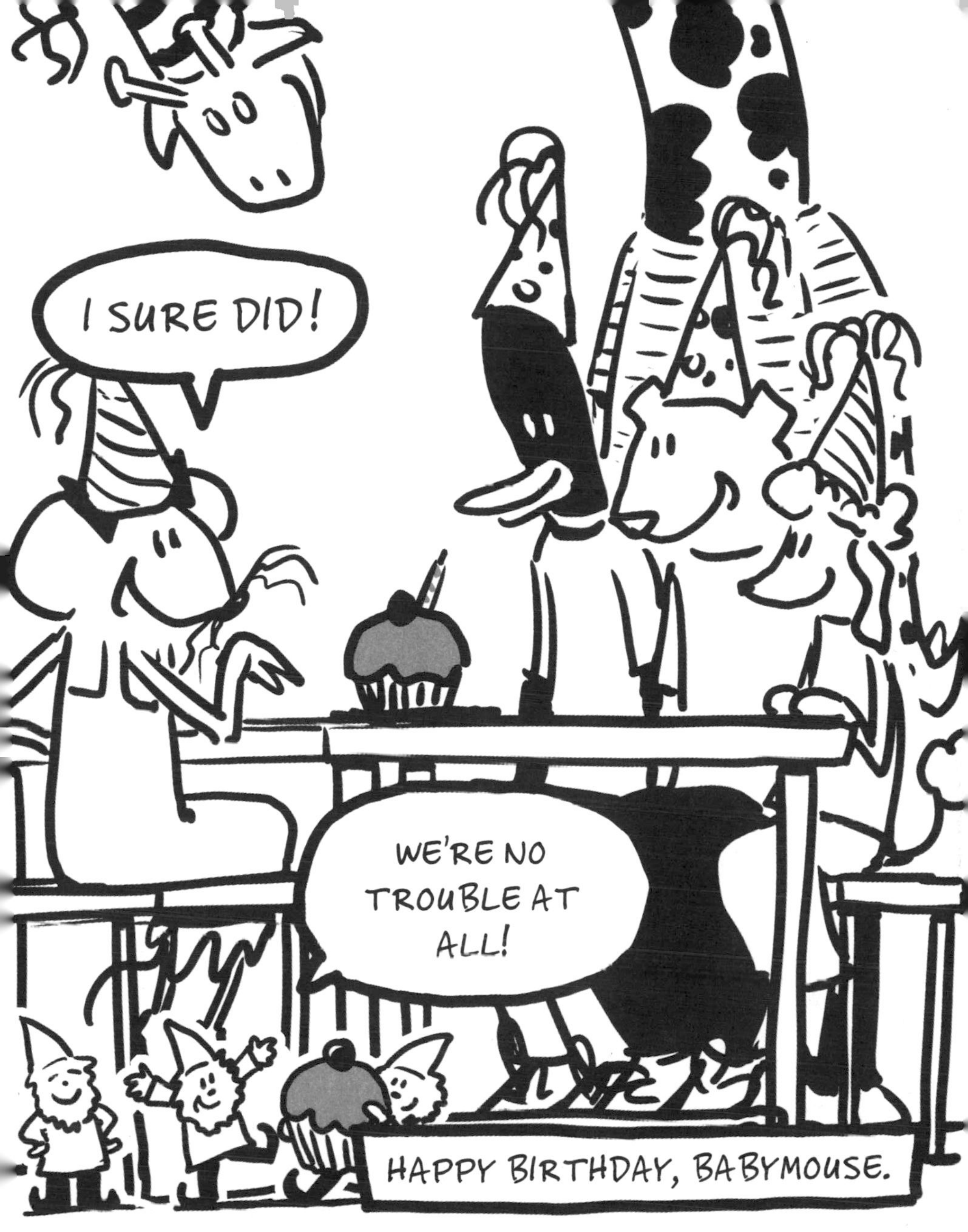
I SURE DID!
WE'RE NO TROUBLE AT ALL!
HAPPY BIRTHDAY, BABYMOUSE.

USA

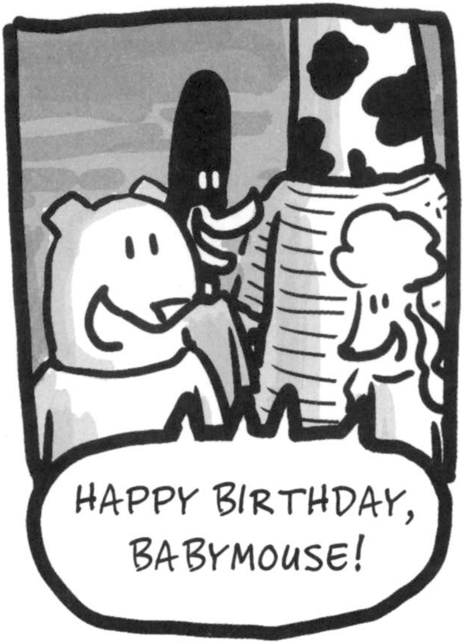
HAPPY BIRTHDAY, BABYMOUSE!

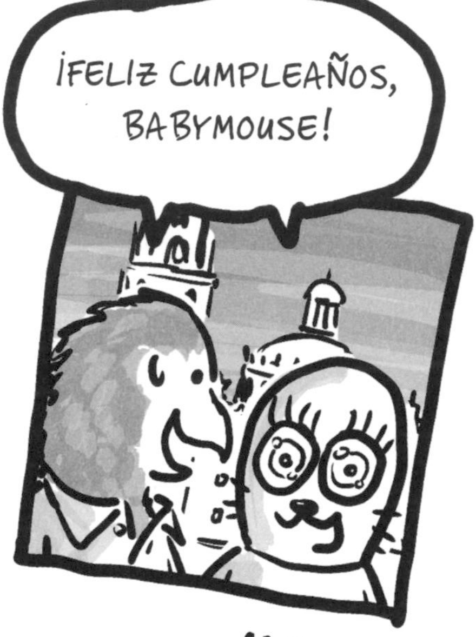
¡FELIZ CUMPLEAÑOS, BABYMOUSE!

MEXICO

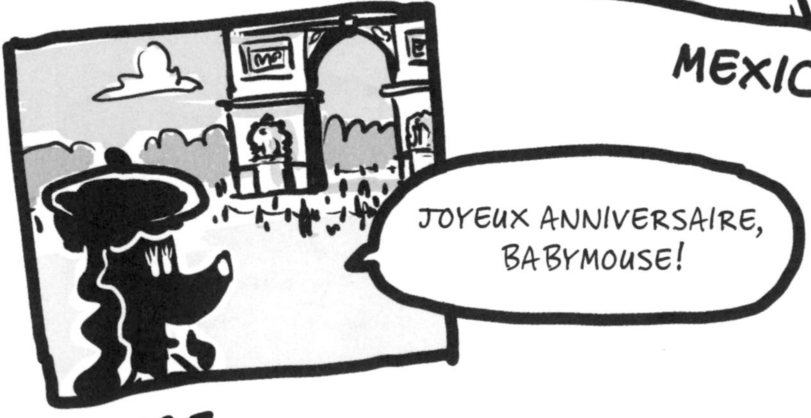
JOYEUX ANNIVERSAIRE, BABYMOUSE!

FRANCE

WORMVILLE

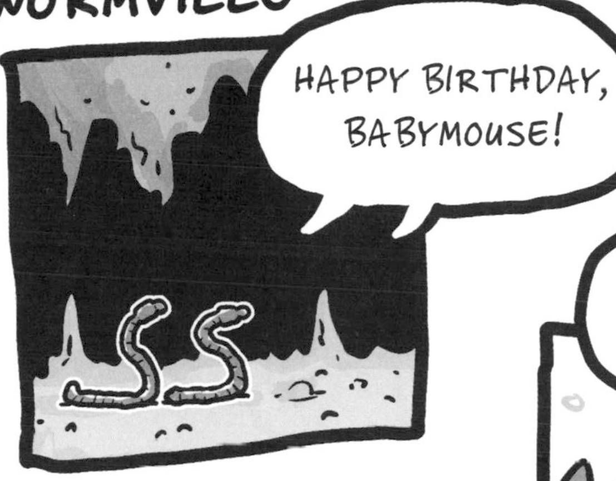
HAPPY BIRTHDAY, BABYMOUSE!

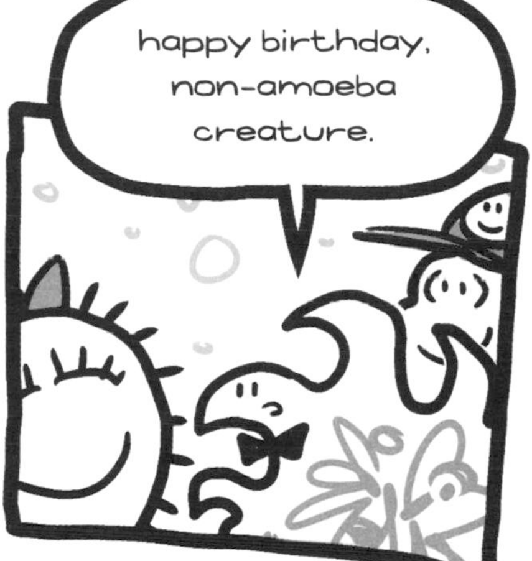
happy birthday, non-amoeba creature.

THE POND

ALPHA CENTAURI

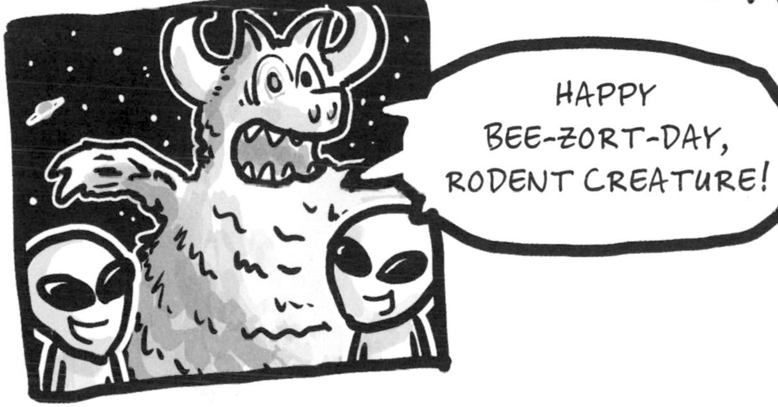
HAPPY BEE-ZORT-DAY, RODENT CREATURE!

BABYMOUSE BONUS!

•LEARN HOW TO DRAW THE ALIENS•

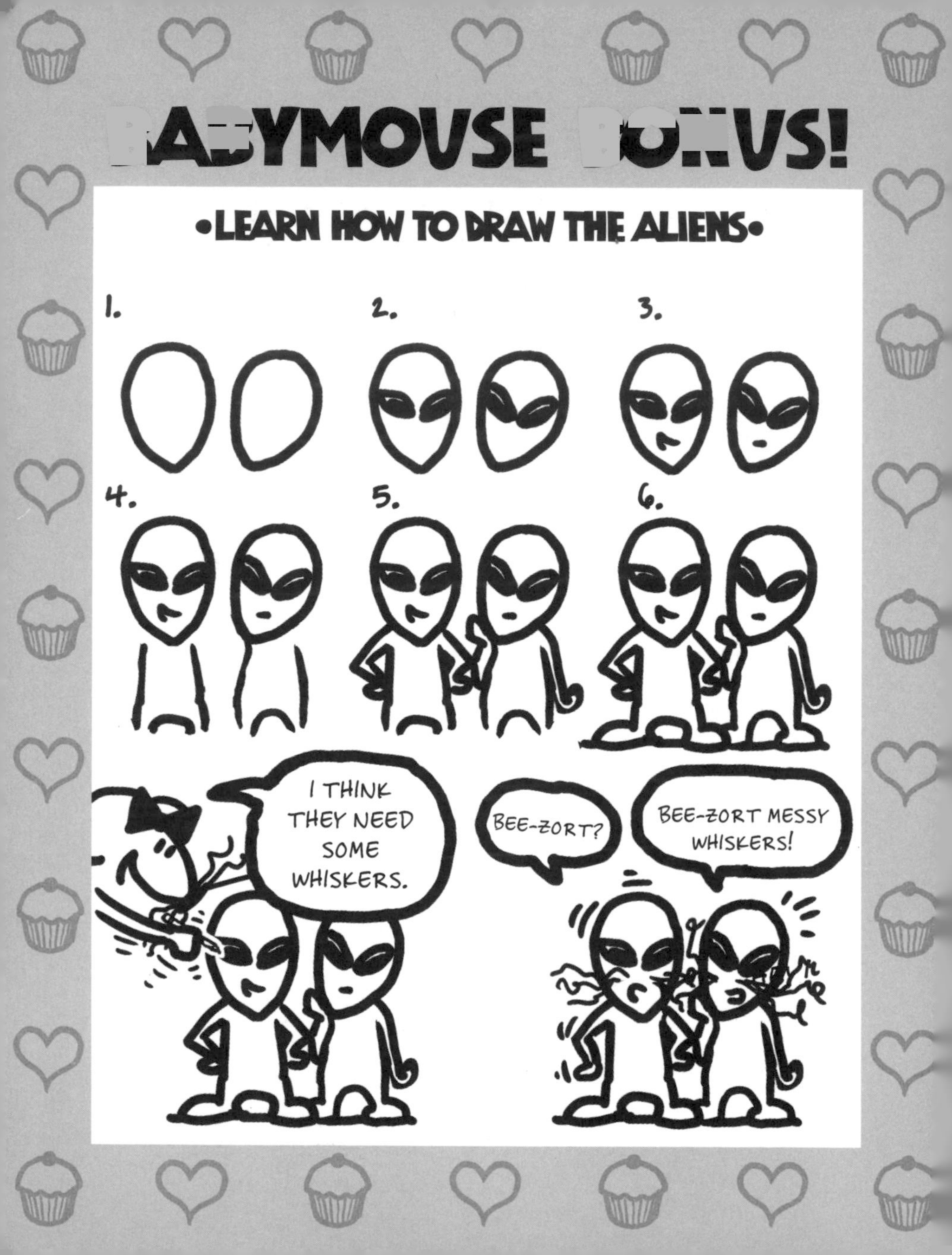

1.
2.
3.
4.
5.
6.
I THINK THEY NEED SOME WHISKERS.
BEE-ZORT?
BEE-ZORT MESSY WHISKERS!

BABYMOUSE BO US!

•FILL IT IN AND MAKE YOUR OWN COMIC•

The search for cupcakes was long.

Even the most faithful cupcake lover lost hope.

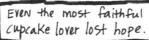

Will we _ever_ find cupcakes?

I think I see frosting over the next ridge.

Text by Jenni Holm

GO TO **BABYMOUSE.COM** TO DOWNLOAD A COPY OF THIS PAGE WITH **BLANK** WORD BALLOONS, THEN FILL IT IN WITH YOUR OWN STORY!

If you like Babymouse,
you'll love these other great books
by Jennifer L. Holm!

THE BOSTON JANE TRILOGY
EIGHTH GRADE IS MAKING ME SICK
MIDDLE SCHOOL IS WORSE THAN MEATLOAF
OUR ONLY MAY AMELIA
PENNY FROM HEAVEN
TURTLE IN PARADISE

AND DON'T MISS THE **SQUISH** GRAPHIC NOVELS BY MATTHEW HOLM AND JENNIFER L. HOLM:

#1   SQUISH: Super Amoeba

#2   SQUISH: Brave New Pond

#3   SQUISH: The Power of the Parasite

#4   SQUISH: Captain Disaster

#5   SQUISH: Game On!

And coming soon:

#6   SQUISH: Fear the Amoeba

NOV 1 9 2014

Roseville Library

Hi! I'm Squish—
I'm an amoeba.
I like Twinkies and comics.
And I'm not really pink,
I'm green.